THE CORRESPONDENCE ARTIST

a novel by
BARBARA BROWNING

This book was printed and bound in Canada by Friesens Corporation. It uses vegetable-based ink on acid-free FSC certified paper.

ENVIRONMENTAL BENEFITS STATEMENT

Two Dollar Radio Movement LLC saved the following resources by printing the pages of this book on chlorine free paper made with 100% post-consumer waste.

TREES	WATER	SOLID WASTE	GREENHOUSE GASES
14	6,220	378	1,291
FULLY GROWN	GALLONS	POUNDS	POUNDS

Calculations based on research by Environmental Defense and the Paper Task Force. Manufactured at Friesens Corporation

For R. Miller

TWO DOLLAR RADIO is a family-run outfit founded in 2005 with the mission to reaffirm the cultural and artistic spirit of the publishing industry.

We aim to do this by presenting bold works of literary merit, each book, individually and collectively, providing a sonic progression that we believe to be too loud to ignore.

All images used with permission.
Photo credits: Cover image uses part of *Portrait of Gertrude Schiele* by Egon Schiele; Author photograph by Jonathan Conklin; pp. 29, 167, Raul Vincent Enriquez (who graciously granted permission); pp. 41, 69, 79, Barbara Browning; p. 95, photo of Richard Schechner's *Dionysus in '69*, property of Richard Schechner (who graciously granted permission); p. 97, photographer unidentified; p. 159, Leo Oliveira (who graciously granted permission).

www.TheCorrespondenceArtist.com

TWO DOLLAR RADIO
Books too loud to ignore
www.TwoDollarRadio.com
twodollar@TwoDollarRadio.com

"'All characters in the following narrative are fictional, not real – but so are the characters of most of the people I know in real life, so this disclaimer doesn't amount to much…'"
—Slavoj Žižek, quoting a certain uncredited "Slovene author"

In fact, certain explicit references are made to real public figures in the following narrative, but all actions and quotations attributed to them are entirely fictional, as is the rest of the story.

THE
CORRESPONDENCE
ARTIST

CHAPTER 1: COCA-COLA AND VIOLENCE

I t isn't easy to be the lover of a great artist – particularly if you harbor any ambition of being an artist yourself. I once jokingly wrote to the paramour, "I'm the Nelson Algren to your Simone de Beauvoir."

Perhaps you know the story of their love affair. Simone de Beauvoir went to Chicago for a speaking engagement, and Nelson Algren was the down-on-his-luck Midwestern novelist who showed her around town. They ended up having an affair and Algren suggested maybe she could move to Chicago to be with him. Of course she told him she couldn't possibly give up her life in Paris with Sartre. But she did like to travel with Algren through foreign countries, and she enjoyed corresponding with him in her slightly flawed English. She found him appealing because he was so American, so unquestioningly leftist, and simultaneously very modest and yet hungry for life. She also liked their sex.

This was very much the appeal I held for the paramour.

I think I can honestly say that I am a woman of extreme moderation. Some people find this attractive. I am neither old nor young. I'm good-looking but not remarkably so. I'm a professional writer – which is to say I make a living as a freelance journalist, and I plug away half-seriously at my poems and, as you can see, the occasional work of fiction. I am a sensitive, intuitive critic, but my own voice has a certain Midwestern flatness about it. Perhaps you've already noticed that.

I'd love to convince myself that my politics are radical, but I'm afraid a more cynical observer might label me a guilt-ridden white liberal. I'm aware of my complicity in the quagmire of global politics. In an attempt to make amends, I give a significant portion of my income to progressive charitable organizations. I sew most of my own clothes, or buy them second-hand. I'm fairly obsessive about recycling. You get the picture.

I am a very dedicated friend and correspondent. Actually, that's probably my real talent. I'm what you might call a correspondence artist.

I'm also a single mother. Sandro is fifteen, and while his temperament mirrors mine in many ways, he's more extreme: extremely tall, extremely thin, extremely beautiful, extremely left-wing, extremely pretentious. He's an expressive, lyrical pianist, but he has a dry sense of humor. Our domestic rapport is, on the whole, very harmonious. This is probably why I've remained single all these years. Sandro's father, Carlo, went back to Italy when Sandro was a baby. I had a series of lovers, some of them long-term, all of whom Carlo denigrated as "losers." I said, "So Carlo, what about you?" He said, "I was the biggest loser of them all. Obviously, you need to feel superior." It was hard not to concede this point to him.

He didn't know, however, about the paramour. It's the only time in my life I've been involved with someone so far above my station in life. Actually, it's the only time I've been involved with somebody solvent, let alone rich and famous. Obviously, these weren't really qualities I was looking for in a lover. I've been very discreet about this, though it's been going on for three years. I think it might be petering out. Since we live on different continents, our love affair has mostly been constituted by e-mail exchanges. At times, our obsession with this process has seemed entirely mutual. At other times the paramour seems to get distracted. My dedication has been unflagging. It's partly fueled, I'm embarrassed to say, by the vain and yet stubborn belief that my overly informative and yet occasionally insightful missives might be feeding the creative process of a genius. I'm probably entirely mistaken. Sandro knows, of course, and he observes the relationship with wry detachment. This attitude helps me to remain detached as well. Sandro finds the whole thing mildly amusing, except when a pause in the correspondence makes me irritable.

Saturday, March 29, 2008, 8:07 a.m.
Subject: I'm irritated with you

If it's laziness, it doesn't cost so much to write to say, "I'm busy/exhausted/taking care of my kids/screwing a lot/having a neurotic crisis – I'll write you in a week."

If it's that fort/da game ("I'm going to push her away so she won't love me too much") it's megalomaniacal.

I woke up thinking this way. Maybe it's my hormones, but only partly.

That was an unusually blunt message for me to send. I think it signaled the beginning of the end. Or maybe the end began well before that. It seems clear that if I'm going to tell this story, this is the moment at which I need to tell you how I came to meet the paramour. But for obvious reasons, this is a complicated proposition – in fact, more complicated than you might think. Fame contaminates things. There are people who stand to profit from the most trivial information about my lover, and other people who stand to lose. So let's pretend it's Tzipi Honigman, the beautiful 68-year-old Israeli novelist who's just won the Nobel Prize.

In December of 2004, I wrote a review for *The Nation* of what I consider to be her most deeply affecting novel, *Embracing*

Anomalies. Of course, the Nobel followed the enormous critical success of her most recent book, *Problems are Defiant like Unattractive Angels,* and this may in fact be the superior work, but that earlier novel really changed the way I understood the power of figurative language. It was full of extended metaphors. It worked like a drug on me. By the end I didn't know anymore what the difference was between narration and figuration. It was trippy (sometimes behind her back I call her affectionately Trippy Honigman), it was sensual – but because of the context there were political ramifications. Fighting against the overwhelming tide of political violence, poetry was like a persistent, muscled swimmer that would reach the shore. Yet amazingly, she was never sentimental.

My review was appreciative, but more than that, it kind of took Tzipi's ball and ran with it. It was probably overwritten. I was inspired, or maybe I was infected. Anyway, Tzipi read it, and she liked it. She sent me an e-mail thanking me. She said that sometimes as a writer you don't really know what you're doing, and it was very gratifying when someone else understood you better than you had understood yourself.

When I found this e-mail in my inbox, I freaked out. You can imagine. I think I was her greatest fan. I think I still am. I called my friend Florence and read it out loud to her. The message was very long. Tzipi praised the brevity of my sentences, and apologized for her own, which she said had a tendency to snake around the page until they ended up swallowing their own tails. Another extended metaphor. She said she hoped we could talk more one day about writing. There was a strange and disconcerting line about another article of mine she thought she remembered reading which made an "antipathetic" comment about her. When I read this, my heart fell with a thunk – I knew what she was referring to, but I certainly hadn't thought of it as a slight. In a review of another Israeli writer's short story collection, I'd made passing reference to Tzipi's stature in the late

'70s as a national icon with something of a "hippie" aesthetic. I didn't consider this antipathetic. I like hippies. But Tzipi's style has certainly accrued a lot of elegance since then.

Florence didn't think I needed to worry too much about Tzipi feeling slighted by that hippie comment. Her message was very warm. Florence said, "You know, I think Tzipi Honigman is the most beautiful woman in the world. She makes you think there's nothing sexier than a woman in her 60s." This is true.

I wrote Tzipi back telling her how honored I was to receive her message, and I hastened to assure her that I'd been a devoted fan for many years. I explained that "hippie" indicated, for me, certain social values which I found myself missing more and more, particularly given the current political climate. I knew she'd agree with me about this. I said that the next time she came to New York, I'd love to cook her dinner. We exchanged one more round of brief messages in which she returned the invitation, should I find myself for any reason in Tel Aviv.

Perhaps you can imagine what happened a few months later. Sometimes one's life feels like a book that's being written by somebody else. I got a freelance gig writing a short piece for a travel magazine: nightlife in the age of anxiety in the Israeli metropole. I'd be spending two nights in Jerusalem, and two in Tel Aviv. I sent Tzipi an e-mail and she wrote me back right away asking what hotel I'd be staying at. She suggested she pick me up on the evening of my first night there, and she'd take me to the famous restaurant Mul-Yam. The chef was a friend of hers. She said if I were going to be out prowling the clubs till dawn, I'd better get myself some sustenance in advance. I said I'd love that.

After I checked into the hotel, I took a shower and set my clothes out on the bed. Everybody said Tel Aviv was very laid back, but this was supposed to be a really nice restaurant. I decided to wear jeans, but with a low-cut blouse and some very high-heeled '40s-style platform shoes. I posed for myself in front of the full-length mirror. I changed my shirt a couple of times but ended up going back to my original choice. Tzipi had said she'd pick me up at 8, but at 7:45 she called to say she was going to be a little late. She was apologetic. It was something about her younger son – he wasn't feeling well, and Tzipi had to wait for her ex to get there. She sounded a little flustered.

When she got to the hotel around 9, they called me from the front desk and said I had a visitor. I walked down the steps and saw her standing expectantly in the lobby. Everybody in the place was looking at her. It's not just that she's so beautiful. She's also extremely famous. People here know Tzipi's face, but in Israel, it's ubiquitous – plastered in the window of every bookstore, smiling enigmatically from street placards, flitting with eerie regularity across the television screen. She was exactly as I'd seen her in those photographs – just, perhaps, a little greyer. That famous white streak through her gorgeous, wild hair had spread out further, almost encompassing her face now in a snowy blur, but her eyes were still shiny and black, rimmed, as ever, with kohl. She held her arms out, and we embraced. It felt strangely natural. She had a very slight scent of vetiver. She said, "You look as I knew you'd look. This is exactly as I pictured you."

Everyone in the lobby smiled at us.

In the car on the way to the restaurant, Tzipi apologized for being late. She explained that she was in the process of a somewhat complicated separation. It had been her decision, and her ex was having a difficult time. Tzipi didn't want to make it any more difficult than it had to be for their son. I wasn't sure how to respond to such immediate intimacy, but I told her I understood. She asked me if I had any children, and I told her yes, one.

She changed the topic to my writing. She told me what she'd liked, particularly, about that review. I said that after I'd read *Embracing Anomalies* I'd felt compelled to write a series of prose poems. She laughed and said she always found this an interesting contradiction in terms, although people often used the expression to describe her more fragmented narratives. She asked me if I knew any of my poems by heart, and if I could recite one to her.

With my heart in my mouth, I did – an unrhymed sonnet about failed love. It was called "Obscene." She looked over at me, smiling just a little. I felt extremely naked.

Everyone knew Tzipi at the restaurant. The famous chef, Yoram Nitzan, came out to speak with us. She told him to bring us whatever he thought was best. Nitzan grabbed her strong brown hand and kissed it. He turned to me and smiled. He said, "You know, we have the best wine list in Tel Aviv – we have our own label, excellent, but Tzipi is horrible, she insists on ruining my beautiful food by washing it down with Coca-Cola!"

It's true. Despite the fact that she is unarguably the most elegant woman in the world, Tzipi Honigman never touches wine. She drinks Coke, assiduously. She said, "There's nothing like a Coca-Cola with a tender piece of foie gras! You don't believe me, but you haven't tried it. I can't tolerate alcohol – it makes me feel desiccated. But I don't prohibit others. Feel free to order wine if you like! Or whiskey!"

I was nervous enough. I didn't think I needed to be the only one impaired. I just asked for mineral water.

The food was exquisite, but I had a hard time eating. At one point I looked up at Tzipi and said – and this was entirely unpremeditated – "I'm nervous." I told her, truthfully, how much I admired her, what she'd meant to me, as a writer, as a reader, and for how long. She took this in gracefully, accepting it at face value. Surely she'd heard this many times before.

What happened next was something of a blur. There was a commotion toward the front of the restaurant, and suddenly I was looking up at a tall, beautiful, distracted young woman in a black leather jacket. Her long brown hair was disheveled, her eyes streaked with ruined make-up. She was staring at me in disbelief. Tzipi looked up and said gently, "Hannah…"

"You told me she was some middle-aged journalist! You said this was 'professional'!"

"I am…" I uttered meekly. "It is…" Tzipi said.

"Tell me you don't think she's beautiful!" Hannah screamed. Tzipi stared back dumbly. "Tell me!"

Tzipi said, "Hannah, what you're saying is extremely flattering to her." She didn't seem to notice that this was pretty insulting, but I was a little too disoriented to take offense. Hannah looked at the table between us, littered with plates smeared with remnants of fatty liver and traces of sauce. She decisively grabbed Tzipi's wine glass of Coke and dumped it on my head.

Everyone, everything, froze. I felt a lump in my throat and worried for a second that I was going to cry. I'm not sure why – if it was just a childish reaction to the spoiling of my perfect dinner with Tzipi Honigman, or if I was in that instant intuiting just how inevitably sad overwhelming love always is. Then as quickly as she'd appeared, Hannah went striding out of the restaurant.

The other diners tried very hard not to pay attention. The waiter quietly swept in with some extra napkins, cleared the plates before me and swabbed away the puddle of brown liquid. I dabbed at the top of my head with my napkin. Tzipi looked up at me and said, "I'm sorry. I'm sorry."

I excused myself quickly and rinsed off a little in the ladies' room. I surveyed the damage: surprisingly minor. But my heart was racing. When I got back to the table, the next course had arrived, but I was sure I couldn't eat it. Tzipi explained a little, but I'd already figured it out, as I'm sure you have, too. Tzipi's life with Hannah was something not much talked about in literary circles, though people knew. They'd always been discreet, even after Hannah conceived a child and Tzipi took to calling him, as well, her son.

Tzipi had been married briefly in the '70s and she had an adult son, Asher, with whom she was very close. In fact, they were famously close — and I'd always identified with her because of that, because of my relationship with Sandro. Maybe it's something of a cliché. Like Susan Sontag and her son. I simultaneously romanticize this model, and worry about its pathological implications. Anyway, the parallels were obvious.

Hannah had been introduced to Tzipi as a young student. She was writing poetry and Tzipi took her under her wing. Hannah stopped writing almost immediately, and pretty soon she'd dedicated herself entirely to being with Tzipi. She moved in. A few years later she had Pitzi. I've seen a photograph of her pregnancy. She was so stunningly beautiful. Annie Leibovitz took a portrait of her, smiling beatifically over her perfect, soft breasts, the tendrils of her brown hair falling over her shoulders, her lovely, round belly circled by Tzipi's unmistakably muscular and yet graceful, tanned arm. Tzipi was mostly out of the shot, obscured by Hannah's naked glory, but you could see her pressing her face into the back of her lover's neck.

That was ten years ago. Hannah was 19. Tzipi was 58.

Sunday, March 20, 2005, 10:29 a.m.
Subject: my bad manners

Tzipi, I felt so sad afterwards — for you, and for her. I hope from the bottom of my heart that things get better soon.

I just wanted to tell you that despite the circumstances, it was an immense pleasure to meet you and talk a little.

I also wanted to give you the reference for that CD of Thelonious Monk learning "I'm Getting Sentimental over You." It's "Monk: The Transformer." If you can't find it, tell me, and I'll send it to you.

I survived my last break-up watching Monty Python's Flying Circus on DVD – I recommend it.

I don't know if I should ask your forgiveness for my timidity, or for being so brash as to seek you out in Tel Aviv, and get you into that mess. Then again, my guide book said that in Tel Aviv, there are two things a foreigner never needs to learn to say in Hebrew: "thank you," and "I'm sorry." It said the expression for "excuse me" is literally "get out of my way." This doesn't come so naturally to a woman like me, whose aggression is generally of the passive variety. So I'll just say, Tzipi, sorry.

Yours, V

After Hannah stormed out of the restaurant we tried to re-cover, but Tzipi's cell phone kept going off. The first two times she spoke in a hushed voice, but when it went off a third time she said, "Maybe I'd better just take you back to your hotel. She's having a hard night." Of course I agreed. God knows, I wouldn't have been able to eat, anyway.

In the car driving back, we tried to talk a little about music. Tzipi often writes about jazz, and piano improvisation is a kind of leitmotif in more than one of her novels. I told her about a fabulous CD a friend had given to Sandro of Monk learning a tune. She was intrigued. As I described it to her, I found myself reaching over and touching her arm. I knew what I was doing.

Then we stopped at a light, and Tzipi looked up into the rear-view mirror. "Oh, look at that," she said calmly. "She's following us." I wrenched around and saw Hannah gripping the steering wheel of the car directly behind us. My pulse picked up again. We pulled up in front of the hotel and I thought to myself, "Maintain composure." Tzipi and I leaned in and kissed each other on the cheek. The porter of the hotel was opening the car door. I swung my leg out, began to step out, and suddenly felt a thud on the right side of my head. Hannah was tackling me. I stumbled but managed to stay upright as she yanked at my hair and swung another punch, this time pummeling my left ear. I turned and ran toward the lobby. I heard a scream and looked back. Hannah had pushed up the sleeves of her jacket and was mercilessly clawing at her own arms and howling in my direction, "If you call her again, if you send her another e-mail, I swear to God, I'll kill you! I saw you kiss in the car! I have a photograph! Bitch! Get the hell out of Israel!" Tzipi had rushed out of the car and was trying to hold a thrashing Hannah in her arms. I ran up to my room without looking back.

Tzipi later told me that the hotel security had misunderstood her attempt to calm Hannah down, and thought she was attacking her. They ended up pulling the two of them apart. Fortunately nobody called the cops, but it took some talking before everyone calmed down.

Needless to say, I didn't do any research that night for my article. The next night I poked around a few clubs in the downtown area and got enough to fill my word count. The section on Jerusalem was a little more thorough, but as you'll surely understand, I kind of wrote this piece on automatic pilot.

Tzipi answered my e-mail very graciously. She said it had been a difficult few days after that scene, but that there had also been moments when Tzipi thought she saw a light at the end of the tunnel. She said she liked Hannah very much, and wanted for her to be happy. She said it was funny that I'd expressed shyness, when she so obviously had so much more to feel awkward about.

I was glad to get back to New York. Sandro found this story pretty amusing. "Wow," he said. "Cat fight." I periodically checked my e-mail over the next few days, half-hoping Tzipi would pop back up, but I was mostly getting messages from the Socialist Party USA [spusa] list serve about labor abuses in

Colombia, and a variety of other spam. One evening I found myself writing a poem. I couldn't resist sending it to Tzipi. It was a sestina, called "Coca-Cola and Violence." It was about those e-mails I was receiving from spusa-listserv and Hannah's blow-out in the restaurant. It basically implied we're all implicated in violence, little and big, political and personal, even if we think we're trying to be good.

Tzipi wrote back saying she liked the poem. She'd been confused by the last line, which was a fragment of a torn-up love letter, but she solved the riddle for herself.

* * *

It's funny, writing about Tzipi, I began to fall in love with her. Which I can do, because she's a fictional character. With the real paramour I'm always on my guard. About a year ago I got an e-mail with the not particularly felicitous formulation: "I love you but I'm not in love with you." As you can imagine, I found this disappointing, but when I really thought about it, honestly, I had to answer that I also felt love but I wasn't sure I was in love. I attributed this to the fact that my lover was always holding something back. It's difficult to abandon yourself to passion when you don't feel safe. When I wrote that, the paramour seemed disconcerted, claiming to have fallen in love only once, in childhood. Romantic passion was a kind of foreign emotion, attractive and yet elusive. And the threat of someone else's passionate desire was mortifying – particularly if it involved possessiveness. That seemed like a pretty pointed message.

It's ironic that I've been falling in love with my lover's fictional manifestation, because when we were discussing what it meant to fall in love (this rather unpleasant exchange evolved into a fairly absorbing philosophical back-and-forth), I could only describe it in relation to fiction.

Thursday, June 7, 2007, 2:17 p.m.
Subject: fiction

I knew your answer would begin with several long paragraphs about the political situation. After all this time, I still find your tirades sexy. And lovable.

Oops, I used the word, in adjectival form. I've been trying to avoid it, especially after you told me how American it was, this business of saying "I love you" all the time. But if you can say it why can't I? I do love you, profoundly, but I'm also not sure if I'm in love with you. It's hard to understand, because you would think that if you loved someone and you also felt as much desire for them as I feel for you that that would be what being in love was.

But I think being in love is when you allow yourself to enter into a state of fiction, where you become very vulnerable, completely open, naïve, and naked. The fiction is thinking: "I can only be happy with this person." Of course, your friends always see this for what it is from the outside. They know you could be happy with someone else, if you chose that.

Believing in the fiction of your singular necessity isn't really possible for me, because of your emotional distance. Also, between us, there are all those other kinds of distance – of language, nation, age, social context. Fame. I won't even speak of politics because that's more ambiguous with you. But of course even if you share those things with someone, even if they would seem to correspond to you in so many ways, there are those moments when you realize that they're miles away from you. Even, I'm sure, if they're the same sex.

Anyway, being in love. It's a huge, beautiful luxury. I do it with more facility than you.

2021 8/6

The paramour agreed.

I fell in love almost immediately with Tzipi, but I don't know why I should feel any safer with her than I do in real life. Still, that's not why I've decided to try something else. It's that there are some ways in which she really doesn't correspond to my lover. It's not what you might think. It's the question of politics. So far Tzipi appears to be a progressive intellectual who nonetheless enjoys the comforts of bourgeois celebrity. My actual lover's politics are very complicated. Often extreme. Let's say, in fact, that he's the legendary Basque separatist, Santutxo Etxeberria, also known by his alias from his more notorious activist days, the Arrano Beltza (the "black eagle"), or increasingly, since his falling out with the ETA, Txotxolo ("the dumb ass"). He prefers the latter.

"Wait," you'll say. "I thought you said the paramour was an artist." But he is. Santutxo is one of the few revolutionaries who raised the struggle to an art form. Well, of course, he once would have said that all revolutionary acts are works of art, but even in his youth he secretly knew that that was mostly puffed up rhetoric, and if pressed, he'd confess that every struggle produced an enormous dung heap of bad poetry. Santutxo was another story. He is completely lyrical.

I came to know of him, as most people do, through his blog. There was a link from the official site of the EZLN. They've since taken it down. Santutxo has a sensitive relationship with El Sup. If you think I've had to be discreet about our love affair, it doesn't even begin to approach what he's had to keep under his hat about his friend Marcos. Of course, if this weren't entirely fictional, I really couldn't be revealing any of this. As it is, I still have to resort to these public personae. Even in his private e-mails to me, Santutxo superstitiously insists on referring to his friend by the various versions of his *nom de guerre*. But they go back – way back. Which is why no matter how far Santutxo goes off his rocker, El Sup will always have a place for him in his heart. Of course he can't state this publicly.

For some, Santutxo is a fallen god. I think falling was a relief for him. Marcos understands this better than anyone, which is probably why he's so forgiving. Also because even in Santutxo's most erratic moments – perhaps especially then – he is irresistibly seductive. When I said the paramour was rich and famous, I was putting his possessions in earthly terms. Of course, Santutxo's capital is of another sort altogether: it's the erotic capital of his political commitment, or the political capital of his erotic power, however you want to put it. There's hardly a woman in Euskal Herria who hasn't masturbated imagining his "piercing dart." I'm sure he's figured prominently in plenty of masculine fantasies as well. The Basque have a reputation, as I'm sure you know, for machismo, but Santutxo has always had excellent gender politics, and his sensuality is polyvalent.

Maybe I should explain that "piercing dart" comment, as it's entirely possible you're not conversant with 16th-century Basque poetry. It was Bernat Etxepare, father of Basque literature, who created the figure in his famous poem, "In Defense of Women" ("Emazten Fabore"). The penultimate stanza says:

Jo badeza dardoaz ere gorputzaren erditik,
ainguruiak bano hoboro ezlarrake gaizkirik,
bana dardoa ematurik, zauri ere sendoturik,
bere graziaz ezarten tu elgarreki baketurik.

My loose English translation from the standard Castilian rendering, accommodating for rhyme and meter, would be:

Although he stabs her tender body with his piercing dart,
She answers him compliantly, as with an angel heart,
And once the dart's relaxed again and stillness seals the part,
She heals them both with gentleness, her reconciling art.

You wouldn't exactly call this a "feminist" poem by contemporary standards, but I find it kind of poignant. There's something so pathetic about the masculine dart-wielder – the way the woman has to take care of him once he's just limp and spent.

Santutxo recited this entire poem to me once on his terrace. I don't speak Basque but I love the way it sounds, especially in his warm, slightly scratchy, incredibly intimate voice. That night the moon was almost full, and Santutxo's place has a beautiful view of the city. I had this flash of self-consciousness – I was in Donostia, alone in the moonlight in the arms of the Arrano Beltza, who was reciting the poetry of Etxepare into my ear as he pressed his hard-on up against my body. He smelled faintly of sweat. How many thousands, how many hundreds of thousands of women and men had dreamt about a scene like this with him? How did I come to find myself here?

But before I tell you that story, I probably need to tell you how Santutxo came to find himself here – that is, there, in his lair, alienated from both the State and from the revolutionary cause to which he'd committed so many years, so much blood, so much heartache, so much poetry.

"We start from humiliation when we write in Basque. It's the darkness that pushes us." – Bernardo Atxaga

It may surprise you to learn that Santutxo didn't grow up speaking Basque. But his father was a man of letters, and he collected, analyzed, and translated early Basque documents, including those of Etxepare. As a young kid, Santutxo couldn't be bothered. But when he was ten years old everything changed. It was 1961, and the ETA had been in covert existence for two years. Some of the founders were former students of Santutxo's father. Of course as a family man, he wasn't directly involved in any actions. He had no advance knowledge (Santutxo's sure of this) of the attempt to derail that train full of Civil War veterans. Perhaps you know, this was the ETA's first major operation, and it failed. That didn't stop the police from raiding Santutxo's house and taking his father in for interrogation. He came home missing four teeth. What's worse, they confiscated and destroyed a valuable 17th-century manuscript he'd been keeping under his bed.

Is it really so surprising that seven years later, Santutxo's cell carried out the murder of Melitón Manzanas? Not even his family knew. Despite everything that had happened, Santutxo's parents remained doubtful regarding the strategy of violent intervention. For five years, Santutxo kept up the appropriate bookish profile, acquiring his *licenciatura* in philosophy. He met Amets, no surprise, in a seminar on Marx, and they became lovers. When the shit hit the fan in '73, they fled together to Mexico City. She had an uncle there who was willing to help them out.

Santutxo enrolled in the doctoral program at UNAM. Amets did too, but she dropped out after the second week with debilitating nausea. She was pregnant, of course, with Aitor. When Franco died two years later, they were gravely tempted to go back, but now, with a kid, it was more complicated. Santutxo thought he might be able to do just as much from Mexico. He had a ham radio, and late at night he'd help strategize new operations with his comrades. Sometimes he'd read out inspirational communiqués, which they'd record and distribute. It was during this time that they started calling him the Arrano Beltza.

When he finished his degree at UNAM, Santutxo was invited to stay on as a lecturer, and it was in his first course that he met the young student on whom he would have such a profound impact. Of course, students can also shape the lives of their teachers. It wasn't just the endless conversations about Gramsci that they shared. It was the soccer skirmishes, the late nights spent listening to cassette tapes of Coltrane, the outings to the *jardin zoológico* with Aitor. It was even Amets.

Santutxo wrote me about this in a long e-mail about sexual jealousy. He claimed he'd never felt it, or rarely. I told you his gender politics were excellent. But I'm not sure you could attribute this attitude entirely to his politics. He was, he explained, constitutionally monogamous, despite his fundamental rejection of the model of the bourgeois marriage, which had historically enslaved women. But he had no desire to constrain the desires or pleasures of any woman. He and Amets lived together in an almost embarrassingly tranquil pattern of affectionate and satisfying, faithful nightly coitus for twelve years. Amets had the occasional romp with a friend, but it was more to affirm her political passions than anything else. I mean her sexual politics, but there was also the erotic draw of rebellion – of course. Who am I to judge? God knows I would have slept with the future Subcomandante Insurgente.

Anyway, when Santutxo set up house with Luz in 1989, it was the same deal: fourteen years of almost exclusively simple, happy, dedicated one-on-one fucking. Not to say that he and I ever had this kind of arrangement. When our preoccupation with each other started to feel uncomfortably binding, we'd shake it off by sleeping with somebody else. We were always feeling each other out, sniffing at each other like nervous dogs, getting close to something and then recoiling. Obviously, there were certain risks for me – from the Spanish authorities, the ETA – and of course there was that incident with Luz. Maybe the stakes for him were even higher. I was used to a fairly rapid rotation, but when Santutxo chose a partner, he had a tendency to stick. If he made a decision, he was going to have to live with it. Cautious, we were lovers, but not committed.

I keep wondering what verb tense to use. The past tense feels a little too definitive. It's not yet clear it's completely over. But as you can see, I've never been entirely sure to what degree it had even begun.

Thursday, April 7, 2005, 1:28 p.m.
Subject: yes it was an unfinished

sentence - a ripped up letter. I probably shouldn't confess this, but whenever I write something, when I'm done I sit up in bed and read it out loud to myself. The ripped up letter was the only part of the poem that was completely fictional, but when I read it to myself, that was the line that made me cry. I didn't know if a man or a woman had written it. The obvious end of the sentence, "no consigo vivir sin tu," is "amor", but I don't think that's how it ended. Maybe it was "cuerpo", or "sexo", or "olor". Anyway, the fact that this word was missing was what made me cry, I think.

Your written voice in English is like your speaking voice in English - elegant, practically flawless, and slightly formal. I enjoy the strangeness very much.

I had to go to Providence, Rhode Island for a professional meeting. To pass the time in the train, I knit a big, warm woolen scarf. I would like to give it to you although I can't imagine when you'll need it. I was very honored that you stopped to notice that the sestina was structured like my article. Maybe you also can see that they both owe something to "The Communiqué on the Sentencing of José Barrionuevo."

The weather is beautiful here. Sandro just discovered Cervantes.

I hope you are well. I send you a kiss.

V

Santutxo had figured out for himself the open-endedness of the last line of the sestina. He liked the poem, and had noted that the almost obsessive, repetitive structure echoed some of my writerly maneuvers in the first article I'd written about him – the one that had brought us together. I should perhaps be embarrassed to say that it was Sandro who got me interested in the Arrano Beltza. It was when he was in the 6th grade at a very progressive alternative public school here in Manhattan. His humanities teacher was a young, earnest member of the Green Party named Wesley. He wore sandals even in the winter. He wore a flak jacket. Wesley had asked the class to do reports on "activist role models." Sandro had some disdain for the poor drudges who could only come up with Martin Luther King and Gandhi. Not that there was anything wrong with them, of course, but he felt he should be looking a little further afield. El Sup was a step in the right direction. And then he found that link to Santutxo's page of communiqués.

It was a goldmine. Soon he had me tethered to the computer as well. There were MP3s of his original ham radio broadcasts, as well as more recent recordings he'd made in English and Spanish. Several of them made our eyes well up with tears. One was so funny we nearly peed in our pants. I did a little internet research on him. Of course, I figured what I was finding was entirely unreliable. It had to be. Each account seemed to contradict another. The individual communiqués, too, were really difficult to dissect. He had a lyrical style that was captivating, but the metaphors were often so attenuated that you ended up losing track of the argument, and suddenly found yourself in utterly unexpected territory. Like a freaky paean to Ronald Reagan.

Santutxo, naturally, posted no photographs of himself, but an image search turned up plenty of snapshots on tribute pages. There were a few from his college days at Deusto, with a floppy mop of black curls, a cigarette dangling from his full lips – Dionysian. Then others from the early '80s in Mexico City – shorn, with a knit cap and a couple days' growth of beard, speaking into the microphone of the ham radio. Another was carefully posed, in front of the flag bearing the eagle image that had become his moniker. The most recent one I found must have been taken in the mid-'90s. There were traces of grey at his temples, but he was still wiry, tanned, and he flashed an impish smile. I can tell you without exaggeration, he is the most beautiful man in the world. When I showed his picture to Florence, she had to agree.

That's not, of course, why I ended up writing a profile of him for *The Paris Review*. It was a short piece about the small but steadfast cult that remained devoted to his missives, despite their erratic shifts in political perspective. I wrote that the compelling thing about his writing was that it was "theoretical and sensual, ironic and lyrical, bitter and sweet, all at the same time." I hypothesized that it was due to this unlikely combo that even those who remained true to the revolutionary ideals he'd apparently disavowed continued to be seduced by his language. Of course, not everybody was susceptible. The official stance of the ETA was "Txotxolo"'s excommunication. That's funny, I just realized what an interesting word that is, *excommunication*. That's the kind of thing he loves to think about. How words spill out in all directions, etymologically, historically, cosmologically, politically. He'll wring a single word out like a wet towel – you can't believe what he can get out of three syllables. We had an exchange that lasted for a week about "denigrate."

My article in *The Paris Review* probably suffered from what the New Critics referred to as the Imitative Fallacy. In fact, my e-mails probably do too. It's hard not to let that kind of thing rub off on you.

Santutxo's English is excellent, if a little stiff. He likes to ask me about obscure words, and also certain slang expressions. He likes dirty words. Last year there was a glitch in our correspondence because the spam filter in my e-mail server had trapped a message with the word "cunt" in it. He wanted to ask me about it. The word, I mean, but he was also asking after my cunt. He told me he wished I'd use more words like that in bed with him. Just to show you what an unusual person he is, he asked me in the same message if we spelled hubris "hybris."

After I discovered the filtered message in the spam folder, I answered it.

Wednesday, October 3, 2007, 9:54 a.m.
Subject: dirty words

Dirty words in English: I could say these things in bed with you, but it would be a little theatrical (I have nothing against theater) because I'm pretty discreet this way and always have been. Florence finds my erotic poems transcendent, she loves the fact that I only use the word "sex" to refer to genitals, masculine or feminine. I think I say "cock" every once in a while. Pussy is an unsatisfactory word, either too debasing or too silly. Cock is sexy. Dick is ridiculous (it's in the middle of the word ridiculous, that might be part of it, but it's also a silly name for a man, as is Willy).

There are no good words for vagina. Including vagina. Penis is clinical and silly but kind of charming. Vagina is just clinical and weirdly noble and distant. When I was 22 I was sleeping with a boy you would have found very beautiful, he worked washing dishes in the restaurant under my apartment, his name was Jorge, he was very delicate, he loved me, and one day we were walking through the park and he stopped with me beneath a tree and said, "Feel my penis." He wanted to show me his hard-on. I thought it was so charming he used this word.

Fuck is a good word. Funny that these words - fuck, dick, cock - are all short and end with -ck. Sharp words, kind of violent.

Screw has a bad sound, but the image is nice. Slow and circular movement. I like it because I like to screw like that. But the word, like I said, isn't great.

I sent you those love letters between Gertrude Stein and Alice B. Toklas. They invented words for all these things. "Tender Buttons" were nipples. You must know that.

Masturbate is not a word I like particularly. I think I wrote you once that I made love to my whole body thinking of you. I know you don't like the phrase "to make love" but it was an accurate description. When I masturbate I'd rather make love to my whole body. Make it a project, something ambitious, something beautiful. Not always, but sometimes I like to do that. It doesn't have to be big – just attentive, careful.

I love chamber music – I often listen to the Bach cello suites. I don't generally like to listen to orchestral music. I am a very focused person.

It made me happy that you imagined me licking your cock. If you were here, if you would let me, I would push you back on my bed and take your cock in my hands and the tip of it in my mouth and I would lick and kiss it and move my hands around the base of it and my cunt would be wet (cunt is a good word! cunt is spelled "cynt" in Chaucer! oh, and we spell hybris "hubris") my cunt would be wet and tight and hungry for you and while I kissed the tip of your cock I'd slip two fingers inside my cunt and feel it tighten until I couldn't wait any more and I'd climb on top of you and take you inside of me and I'd kiss your mouth and the kiss would be hot and my breath would be fast and shallow in your mouth and I'd come, I think, immediately.

And afterwards I'd hold you inside of me and you'd feel me throbbing like that.

Wouldn't that be nice?

His response began, "Oh I love cunt." He went on to defend the word *dick*, and then launched into a fairly cranky complaint about my claim to being "focused," which he interpreted as accusatory. We'd recently been debating the question of focus in sex. I had expressed some doubt about three-person couplings, to use an oxymoron. He'd reported recently engaging in such an event. Let's face it, these opportunities arise with some frequency for a man like Santutxo. Revolutionary sex symbols arouse all kinds of communal ideals in people. I said I had nothing against this in principle, but that in practice it struck me as overly distracting.

Santutxo's answer was, as I said, cranky, and also lengthy and self-contradictory. After passionately arguing for the potential for "focus" while fucking two women, he went off again on the debilitating, anti-feminist fiction that many women clung to, associating sexuality with the bourgeois marital ideal. Still, he reiterated his constitutional tendency toward constancy with a single partner, as evidenced by his two lengthy and largely uninterrupted runs with Amets and Luz. I was surprised to have touched a nerve with that brief reference to focus, despite the obvious affability of the rest of my e-mail. I said, "After I wrote you last I thought maybe you'd just write back, 'Yes, that would be nice.' I mean about me sucking your cock, and slipping it into my cunt." He said, "You found my message cranky? But it began, 'Oh I love cunt.'" I said I might have found that warmer in tone if it had contained the possessive pronoun "your." I said "I love cunt" sounded like a t-shirt that Sandro might wear (Sandro, like Santutxo, is a committed feminist whose way of expressing it might not always read as such). He thought my desire for a personal pronoun was further evidence of a politically suspect individualism – very "American."

* * *

Obviously, I've fallen prey to Santutxo's seductive powers, but it's also embarrassingly clear that in making him up, I've exaggerated the paramour's political sacrifices. Even I need a break from this farce. I also experienced a painful twinge of self-consciousness when I realized I'd just approximated the paramour to my son. I'm afraid it's time to grapple with the uncomfortable fact that my lover is closer to a state of adolescent naïveté than you might find appropriate for a woman of my age and experience. One way to configure this would be to tell you, outright, that he's the 22-year-old art world phenomenon, Duong Van Binh.

Sunday, May 11, 2008, 11:14 a.m.
Subject: miniature golf

I loved "Cage was half miniature golf, half wailing castrato." But the next sentence, "It's genius to contain such disparate impulses," is totally narcissistic seeing as you wrote it. But true.

Walter is my brother, the one you met. HE'S the one who broke his arm falling on the miniature golf course. He likes a lot of things like that – laser tag, truck pulls, bowling - he's also one of those people who drinks a gallon of Sprite when he goes to the movies. But the music he listens to is that doleful, melancholic, obscure indie rock you spoke of.

I'm reading The Mandarins. And some books about Tel Aviv, Hanoi, Bamako, El Sup, and the history of the ETA. Research. You didn't say whether you read that essay by Lethem.

Hm. The writing of this chapter was interrupted by my receiving a message from the paramour, and I felt compelled to respond. This strikes me as an unfortunate glitch. I had written first, it's true, but just because I needed to communicate a small piece of practical information, and I happened to mention, in passing, that my brother had broken his arm under unfortunately silly circumstances. Typical for the paramour to have forgotten my brother's name, even though they've met.

The whole point of beginning this novel, of course, was to displace my excessive interest in the correspondence into a piece of writing of my own. This way, instead of waiting impatiently for ever-dwindling dribs and drabs from my lover, I could just plug away on my own. It's been working pretty well. In fact, I started to find myself waking up hoping for no messages in my inbox, so I could just get straight to the novel, straight to Tzipi, and later Santutxo. But I clearly can't resist stringing the real correspondence along, half-heartedly. Telling a little anecdote, suggesting that essay and so on.

Maybe I'm a little too hard on Binh. What did I expect? The scene of me tethered to the computer with Sandro wasn't inaccurate, but we weren't reading the communiqués of a Basque separatist. We were watching Binh's YouTube postings. Leave it to both Binh and Sandro to be on the cutting edge of these things. It was just a week after the launch of the site, in February of 2005, when Binh uploaded the first in his series of short videos, "zona fasciculata." "Zona glomerulosa" came later, and the "Bartholin's gland" series didn't start until last year. That first video was uncanny. People started passing the link around. As I watched it, I realized it was either brilliant, or very dumb. But its charm was inescapable. Maybe it was age-inappropriate for me to become fixated on Binh's weird, poetic images. Maybe it was because I was living with a teenager. But I thought I recognized a sophistication in his work. The pared-down references to Tarkovsky, the subtly disjunctive Godardian soundtrack – you could tell he knew more than he was letting on. I wrote up a piece for *Wired* magazine, thinking this was just a curiosity. But somebody from *ArtForum* called me the day it went up, and as you know, his reputation spread virally. I can't take any credit for that. Anybody with even a modicum of sensitivity could see that Binh's work was a provocation. People wanted to draw connections – to Nam June Paik, Bruce Nauman, Sadie Benning, Bill Viola, Shirin Neshat – but I found him unique. Of course there were influences. He's incredibly erudite about art history, as well as the history of experimental film, video, sound, and poetics. Some people accuse him of being derivative. And some people, of course, just find him bad. They think his moments of spare minimalism just indicate that he doesn't have that much to say. I found them very touching.

Binh liked my piece in *Wired*. In it, I'd described some of the recurring images in "zona fasciculata" – fleshy, yet abstract; sexual, yet oddly pristine – and I titled the article "Duong Van Binh's Heart on a Plate." I was glad they let me do something kind of lyrical like that. It seemed appropriate. He sent me an e-mail when he read it. There was no text, just an embedded image, beautiful, innocent, saturated with color: a split beef heart on a piece of chipped china.

I was so touched he'd made this image, apparently, for me and me alone. Sandro was very impressed.

Binh was already getting to be a household word among the youthful YouTube cognoscenti, as well as some of the influential curators and critics of my generation. *Interview* magazine asked me to fly out to Berlin to speak with him. He said he was glad it was going to be me.

You may be wondering how I can be flitting off on these international flights with such frequency, given that I'm a single mom. But keep in mind, I'm giving you various fictional versions of a single trip. Still, I must confess, I do leave Sandro home alone with a bit more ease and frequency than some parents might. The first time was that initial meeting with the paramour. Since then, I've done it two or three times a year. Sandro's been completely amenable to this plan. He's so mature. He's so tall. I realize that doesn't mean much. We have a doorman, we're friendly with our neighbors, and both Florence and Walter call and check in on him. I try not to leave him for more than a few days at a time. He eats take-out. I leave him detailed instructions regarding his homework and piano. So far so good.

I texted Sandro on my BlackBerry from the hotel room when I got to Berlin. I said, "Dude I can't believe this hotel room – the bed is on the ceiling." They'd booked me into the Upside Down Room at the Propeller Island City Lodge. Maybe you've heard of this place. Binh had recommended it – it's run by his friend Lars Stroschen. Binh was about to release a CD of his video soundtracks on Lars' label, which puts out experimental sound discs. Lars basically runs his hotel to support the label, which obviously doesn't turn a big profit. Every room in Propeller Island has a theme. In my room, all the furniture was bolted to the ceiling. There were some foam pads you could sit or lie on under the floorboards, but there weren't many convenient places to put your stuff. It was a little disorienting.

Of course there are no televisions at Propeller Island. That was kind of a relief – no temptation to watch CNN or MTV. Depending on your perspective, I guess you could say I was lying above the ceiling staring at the floor when Binh texted me to say he was going to be a little late for our dinner date. That was a good thing because I'd lost track of time and hadn't yet chosen my outfit. I changed my top a couple of times. When I looked at myself in the upside-down mirror, I thought I looked beautiful but it seemed strange that my hair wasn't flying upward toward the floor. When Binh texted to say "im in the lobby," I climbed down the stairwell, running my hands against the wall. By the time I got down there things had righted themselves back to some semblance of reality.

Still, it was a shock to see him standing there, looking at me with such familiarity. He had a faint smile on his face. He was wearing a motorcycle jacket and he held a helmet in each hand. Before handing me mine, he told me I looked exactly as he'd imagined I would. That was an unusually self-possessed thing for someone his age to say to someone like me. Of course, Binh doesn't seem his age. He's one of those people that other people refer to as an "old soul." We were standing very close to each other in the lobby and it was all strangely intimate. It was the first moment I actually articulated to myself that we might sleep together. You might have thought I'd have figured that out from the photo of the bloody heart. I think I was just afraid to want it.

He drove us on his scooter to a Vietnamese restaurant he likes called Monsieur Vuong. It's in the section they call Mitte. It was intensely crowded, but Binh is a regular there and the hostess helpfully ushered us to a corner table in the back. A few people seemed to be watching us as we moved through the crowd. I wondered how many of them realized this was Duong Van Binh. They might just have been looking because he's so astonishingly beautiful.

Binh is of medium height, with glossy black hair nearly as long as mine. His features are exquisitely delicate, almost feminine. His smile is radiant, easy, and entirely natural. I was surprised at how good his English was, as well as his German. He also speaks perfect French, but of course he ordered in Vietnamese. I asked him to order for me, since I don't know a lot about Vietnamese food. He recommended the gói bo. I asked him if Tiger beer was any good and he laughed, saying I was welcome to try it if I liked but that he only ever drank Coca-Cola. On this point he was resolute. The waitress smiled knowingly. I just asked for mineral water.

I guess you know what happened next. There were his appreciative comments on my perceptions regarding his work, the uncanny resonance between our sensibilities, my awkward, spontaneous admission of admiration and of nerves – and in a flash, there was Aafke, coming undone.

After I'd dabbed the Coca-Cola out of my hair in the bathroom with damp paper towels, after Binh repeatedly tried to calm his ex-wife down on the cell phone and finally gave up, after she menacingly chased us back to Propeller Island on her scooter, after that confused scuffle on the sidewalk and my cowardly flight up the disorienting stairs, there I was: trying to pull myself back together from the counter-intuitive gravitational field of that uncomfortable foam pad above the ceiling, while a real bed hovered tantalizingly below me on the floor.

Here's that sestina I sent the paramour after the incident:

Coca-Cola and Violence

Recently I've been inundated with news of allegations that the Coca-Cola
Company has been sponsoring acts of unconscionable violence
Against union organizers at its bottling plants in Colombia. One photo
Shows Isidro Segundo Gil, a union officer, murdered at his workplace. I receive this information by e-mail,

As I'm on a list serve for those with an interest in labor politics. I've never seen

So many messages about a particular multinational case of alleged abuse: at last count, 42.

I'm sure I'm implicated, too.

Not that I've been sponsoring acts of murder, but I've been known to drink a Coca-Cola

On occasion. In fact, it occupies a conspicuous product placement in one scene

Of my life's cinematic version. A dramatic scene, with violins.

A desperate woman is tossing a glass of the stuff on my head, screaming, "If you call again, if you send another e-mail,

I swear I'll kill you! I have a photo!"

I'm not sure exactly what she was going to do with that photo,

Whom she thought she was going to send it to.

Actually, I doubt this photo exists. If it does, maybe she should put it in the mail

To the Colombian bottlers of Coca-Cola.

Wouldn't that just prove, we're all implicated in some kind of violence.

I'm not making excuses for them. I never intended to provoke this scene.

But don't we all play innocent sometimes? That scene

In the restaurant, the murder of Isidro Segundo Gil, some ostensibly platonic embrace captured in a telephoto

Lens outside a hotel in Neve Tzedek – these are not random acts of violence.

There's a horrible mathematical logic to them. The balance of power between two

Married people is as terrifying as the massive economic power of the Coca-Cola

"Family" of products. In some Romance languages, the word
     "Coca-Cola" is female

Although the CEO is quite distinctly male.
His smiling, goofball, gringo mug can also be seen
On the "killercoke.org" website, next to Isidro's. The Coca-Cola
Company probably never imagined this particular use of that
     photo.
The website says Isidro's children "understand too
Well why their homeland is known as 'a country where union
     work is like carrying a tombstone on your back.'" Violence

Begets violence.
It spreads with the exponential virulence of a list serve. My
     e-mail
Is out of control. And in a dimly lit bar in Cebu City, or Abidjan,
     or Bucharest, two
People might be unknowingly on the verge of an ugly scene.
Nobody's there to capture it in a photo.
She's smiling and touching his arm. He's drinking rum and
     Coca-Cola.

Here in my city, in a trash can on Ludlow Street, I found a half-
     empty Coca-Cola and the remnants of an act of violence:
A stained photo, and a ripped-up piece of mail
With the words *no consigo vivir sin tu*

In the three years of our romance, Binh only came once to
see me here in New York. Even that trip wasn't *explicitly* about
seeing me, but there were no other pressing professional obligations to bring him here that time, and it was in a period of
relative demonstrativeness on his part in our correspondence. I

said relative. Of course, there were a few other times he had to pass through quickly for professional reasons – the opening at the Guggenheim (which was where he met Walter), his show at Barbara Gladstone – but these were fleeting and we hardly had a chance to relax. This trip I'm talking about was different. He said in an e-mail before his arrival that this visit would probably be "instructive" for both of us. I didn't ask him to elaborate.

I told Binh he was welcome to stay at our place, of course, which isn't huge – but we do have a little guest bed in an alcove that has a separate bathroom. He likes to sleep in his own bed. He's a physically affectionate person and he loves having sex, but he has a hard time sleeping and he likes to stay up late at night reading. The sound of another person breathing distracts him. He thanked me for the invitation but told me that his friend Naeem had offered him his empty loft in Tribeca. The place was enormous, and beautiful. I couldn't blame him for accepting.

The day he arrived, he texted me and asked me to come over. This was late May of last year. The weather was beautiful, and I walked down West Broadway. When I got there I took the freight elevator up. It opened directly into Naeem's loft. Binh was wearing turquoise silk pajamas. Everything else was white. It was an enormous open space with four columns and stripped wide-planked oak floors. There were a couple of sheep-skin rugs scattered on the floor, and a big white platform bed at a skewed angle near a wall of floor-to-ceiling windows. They were partially opened, and gauzy white curtains billowed over them. It was like being in a cloud. Binh smiled and embraced me wordlessly. He pressed his hard-on up against my body and we began to kiss. He smelled faintly of patchouli. It's always like this when we see each other: we fall into each other's arms and within minutes we're fucking. It's only afterwards, when we've gotten that out of our systems, that we actually talk. That afternoon in the loft was pretty heavenly. He always gets very animated after sex. I'm the opposite. For some reason he wanted to tell me all about

Ozu and interior shots, something he'd been working out about the poetics of space, and it was fascinating but I was having a hard time responding coherently. I was still in a fog of sexual satisfaction. Fortunately he didn't seem to notice. And then he sat up and said, "By the way, do you want to have dinner with my friend Matt and his wife? I forgot to tell you, they asked if we wanted to stop by around seven." It was already six.

It was all right with me. I showered off in Naeem's austere black slate bathroom and climbed back into the slinky orange dress I'd worn. I had a little ziplock bag of edible flowers in my purse. I'd grown them on my balcony, and I brought them thinking Binh might want to eat them in a salad. Now I thought this might be a good gift for this couple. I was intrigued that Binh was taking me to a dinner party, apparently as his date. We hadn't really appeared out publicly together – certainly not as a couple. At this point, partly on account of some media speculation regarding a few famously gorgeous women Binh had been spotted with, there tended to be photographers at his official appearances. This was just dinner with friends, but even in these more intimate contexts, we'd tried to avoid attention. It was partly because of Aafke, of course. I think we both knew some people might consider it a little inappropriate, our being together, but our discretion wasn't about that. I am pretty sure that both of us would adamantly defend the right of any woman or man to find a personal or erotic connection with whomever she or he might choose. But though we were lovers, we rigorously avoided being a "couple." As I said, when it started to feel like we were one, we both had a tendency to recoil.

Binh had forgotten the address but he knew his friend's phone number. He asked me to call from the taxi to get the house number. A woman with a slight accent picked up. Binh hadn't told me her name, so I somewhat awkwardly said, "Hello, this is Binh's friend – we're on our way over but we forgot the address." She told us, and the cab pulled up. We rang the doorbell. Björk opened the door.

Binh, of course, had neglected to tell me we were having dinner with Matthew Barney and Björk. Julian Schnabel was also there. He was telling Matthew Barney a big, evidently funny story when we walked in. He paused when he saw Binh, and came running over to give him a bear hug. Björk was soon affectionately stroking his hair and telling him how well he looked. Binh and Matthew Barney exchanged some kind of special, complicated handshake. They all turned to me politely and smiled when Binh introduced me. I handed Björk the ziplock bag of slightly wilted flowers and said, "These are edible. If you want you can put them in a salad." She was very nice. She ran over to Schnabel and said, "Julian, look, Vivian brought us edible flowers! Here, eat one!" They each took a little limp blossom and chewed on it. They both raised their eyebrows and smiled.

The dinner was very nice. Although he's soft-spoken and his English is a little stilted, Binh likes to tell long stories. Sometimes you wonder where they're going, but in the end there's usually an interesting, unexpected image or a fragment of poetry or something that makes them memorable. Everyone seemed fascinated. Then Björk started to tell an anecdote about her childhood in Iceland, but I noticed that Binh seemed to be spacing out. I think he was listening to the music playing in the background. It was the soundtrack of *Pierrot le fou*. Quite abruptly, he said to our hosts, "Well, thank you very much for this lovely dinner. I think Matt is tired and we should let you get some rest." Schnabel looked surprised, but since Björk and Matthew Barney didn't seem to be objecting, he said he'd walk out with us. We embraced on the sidewalk and Schnabel hailed a cab. Binh walked me home.

Naturally, I've changed the identities of the generous, attractive celebrities at the dinner party. I'm sure Björk is also very nice, but I've never actually had dinner at her house. Why should it matter anyway that you'd recognize their names? Why should I have felt at all out of place that evening, or two days later when Binh and I were flipping through art magazines at Naeem's loft and Lou Reed and Laurie Anderson suddenly buzzed up because they knew Binh was in town and couldn't resist popping by?

Binh stayed in New York for a week, and we saw each other every day, but slept apart. In addition to these purely social visits, he had a few informal meetings with curators and dealers. I tried not to appear overly expectant. He came by our place one afternoon and spent about an hour looking at strange animation sites on the internet with Sandro. Sandro asked him to tag a DVD with a Sharpie. They like each other. Sandro doesn't tell his friends his mother's sleeping with Duong Van Binh. I don't think it's because he thinks it would be unseemly because of our age difference. Sandro and his friends are very open-minded about these kinds of things. I think he just doesn't want to look like he's bragging. Also, I've asked him to be discreet.

I don't know how "instructive" that time of Binh's in New York was.

Monday, June 4, 2007, 7:17 p.m.
Subject: Octopussy

I woke up early. Sandro was HILARIOUS over breakfast. I can't even remember all of it, but he kept calling me Dr. Octopussy and there was something about Spiderman and using his superpowers to increase our wireless capacity. Totally Monty Python.

I have the impression that he was being so entertaining on purpose, so I wouldn't miss you. But I've stopped agonizing over our goodbyes. Maybe I'm getting used to this. I didn't suffer in March, and I feel okay again this time.

I loved seeing you here. I wanted to introduce you to my friends. We only got to see yours. I liked them all. But you would have liked mine, too. That business of finding a common language, I think we still haven't gotten there exactly. You understand I'm not talking about your English, or my French. It's something else.

You're a very complicated person. Sometimes I feel extremely close to you and other times not. You're Ultra-Sensitive, and then not. Sometimes I think your politics are smart and provocative, sometimes I think they're just terrible. Sometimes I find the world of publicity that you inhabit kind of baffling. That business with Kate Moss.

And then there are these other moments. That afternoon at Naeem's when you drew those flowers on my wrist – I'll never forget that, it felt so fragile. In those moments, I understand everything, I feel everything – I just started crying remembering it. Your drawings, your photographs, your videos, the way you understand books and films – there are times when I think that I understand you in a very particular way, that you understand me too. And your tenderness in bed, when we're almost entirely still, that subtle movement, so sweet and at the same time so overwhelming. I love that.

But I think it's good that I also have these little moments of alienation, which you must also have. I told you, I'm trying hard not to like you too much. I want to look you in the eye. I taught you that expression we have. Even Steven.

I found you more beautiful than ever. I love your smell. When I'm near you I can only think about fucking. I can't believe you want to recuperate the image of Ronald Reagan. You even said something nice about Nancy. It's unbelievable.

I'll read the book you gave me and I'll tell you what I think. I'll also tell you when the podcast is done - any day now. Tell me if you read Aciman.

I send you a kiss. V

Maybe I should explain a thing or two. The line about Ultra-Sensitive referred to the condoms Binh likes. I crocheted him a really lovely little condom pouch out of metallic yarn, that just exposes the top of the little square of plastic wrapping where it says "Ultra-Sensitive." I showed him that and said, "Ultra-Sensitive – that's you." He smiled and said, with his very subtle, slightly formal accent, "Not really."

I'd rather not explain right now the line about Kate Moss. I don't have a lot of patience for that kind of thing.

Binh responded to my e-mail, as he sometimes does, with a .mov file. He'd edited it out of some clips of my eyelid that he'd shot while we were together. He did this one afternoon right in the middle of our sex. We'd been having sex, missionary style, which frankly is Binh's favorite, and of course my eyes were shut, but when I opened them I saw that he was looking into them very intently as he pumped up and down. He slowed down a little and said, "Has your right eyelid always been that way?" I asked him what he meant. He said that he'd noticed that my right eyelid was a little lazier than my left. It's funny because I'm vaguely aware of this, but it's not the kind of thing most people would notice. It's very subtle. It's nothing a doctor ever raised with me, or even my mother, for that matter. I asked Sandro later if he'd ever noticed this and he had no idea what I was talking about. The only other person who ever commented on this, sort of, was Florence, who told me when we met in college that she liked to watch my "slow blink." She also liked to watch my lips when I pronounced words that began with the letter *b*. I love Florence.

Anyway, it's true, when I blink there's a very slight lag time between my left and right eyelids. I think it might become slightly exaggerated when I'm in or near a state of orgasm. This may have something to do with Binh's having noticed it. He's also extremely attentive. So right then, in the middle of this, he pulled over one of those somewhat antiquated little eyeball-shaped webcams, and started shooting some very low-resolution, grainy shots of the motion of my slightly retarded right eyelid. We weren't laughing. It was very intimate. It was sexy. At some point later he also pointed that eyeball at my vulva and I think that material came out looking very abstract, and beautiful. But that's not what he sent me. Ultra-Sensitive as he is, Binh wanted to show me we were looking each other in the eye, naked, with all our touching peculiarities. That is, I think this is what he was showing me. This is a still from the .mov file:

I found it very poignant. I felt like no one had ever looked at me that closely.

A few weeks later, however, when he appeared, self-satisfied, on the cover of *Paper* magazine with Chloë Sevigny and Scarlett Johansson licking his stomach, the thought struck me that maybe he was just documenting my imperfection.

* * *

The paramour can, in fact, be pretty unfeeling sometimes. I can't say I wasn't forewarned. I don't just mean that sweetly formal "not really" to my offering of the title Ultra-Sensitive. The initial scene at the restaurant, that placid "what you're saying is extremely flattering to her" – that should have been a dead giveaway. Later, when an e-mail contained a reference to "that beautiful, dumb Thai girl with whom I've been screwing," I had to pause to wonder if anybody were getting messages referring to me as the paramour's "intelligent but only reasonably attractive" American sex pal. Maybe this kind of comment about the Thai girl will make you question the paramour's supposedly excellent gender politics. Sometimes I think that myself, but I don't think it's reducible to machismo. After all, Tzipi says this kind of thing on a regular basis. The question of racial objectification also seems to be threatening to rear its ugly head. I wonder if it will at all complicate things if I tell you that the paramour is the griot superstar, the international dreadlocked dreamboat, the Mick Jagger of Mali, Djeli Kouyaté?

Of course being a "World Music" rock star doesn't inherently guarantee that he wouldn't be capable of racial or ethnic exoticization, just as Tzipi's being a woman doesn't inoculate her from sexism. Lest you think Santutxo's a saint, think again. Or more nearly: it's precisely because he kind of *is* a saint that he feels compelled on occasion to be this crass and selfish. What can you say about a babe-in-arms like Binh? He doesn't even realize what he's doing yet.

"And what about you?" you may be thinking. "What makes you think a Midwestern white woman jetting off to Bamako is immune to any of this either?" Don't think I haven't thought about this myself.

Rolling Stone magazine sent me to do a story on Djeli's homecoming in March of 2005. Actually, he'd requested me. As you know, he'd written me a few months before to thank me for that profile in *The New Yorker*. I'd never met him, but I'd been following his career for some time. His 2004 release, *À Tierno*

Bokar, was one of the most politically trenchant and yet poetically sophisticated albums of recent memory. I don't mean just among "World" artists. You can see I keep putting scare quotes around the term, and I hope you'll understand that it has to do with the absurdity of the commercial bracketing of somebody as profoundly cosmopolitan as Djeli under a term which, despite its cosmic proportions, reads to the consumer as narrowly exotic. At this point, Djeli himself has had the conversation so many times he's bored with it. Anyway, the brilliance of *À Tierno Bokar*, both lyrically and musically, was so self-evident, a lot of music journalists who usually covered other genres picked up on it – rock, jazz, classical. We were all talking about it.

I tend to write about jazz, but because my background's in literature, when I do deal with vocal music and original lyrics I pay a lot of attention. His earlier albums were also layered and complex, but I couldn't think of another disc that had such a novelistic intricacy. I did a very detailed reading. He'd helpfully included his own cross-translations between Bambara, French, and English in the liner notes. Even these translations were tricky, attentive to his own assonance, punning, and percussive metrics. There was a little citation from Amadou Hampté Bâ about orature, and how *"les hommes de l'oralité"* were *"passionnément épris de beau langage et presque tous poètes."* One may have one's doubts about all oral cultures being this rich, but Djeli, without question, is passionately in love with language. He's definitely a poet.

He said mine was the only critique he'd read that actually seemed to understand the full complexity of what he was trying to do. In fact, he said he wasn't sure he'd understood it himself until he read my piece. He can be kind of self-effacing like that sometimes.

Djeli comes from a family of griots, but he went to boarding school in France and then studied philosophy at the École Normale Supérieure. The one in Paris, not the one in Bamako.

He plays kora and electric guitar with equal virtuosity, and he's extended the technique of both instruments correspondingly. He was twenty years old and living in Paris when the coup took place, twenty-one when the democratic constitution went into effect. There were some hopes for him to return to Mali and become active in politics. It was clear that he was to be one of the leading intellectuals of his generation. Ousmane Sembène, the Senegalese filmmaker and writer, took a special interest in him, but encouraged him to follow his artistic impulses. Musically, these ran the gamut from Touré to Satie to Hendrix. Poetically, from the Epic of Sundiata to Verlaine to Dylan.

À Tierno Bokar was a complicated project for him to take on. He'd long ago openly stated his resistance to all organized religion and his specific concerns regarding Islam – not just fundamentalism, but even some moderate forms. He most frequently voiced his concerns in relation to gender politics and homophobia. But obviously, it was also important to acknowledge a figure of tolerance such as Bokar. His sister, Kadidia, was deeply involved in Sufism, and this surely had an influence on the project. So much has been said about that album. It won the Grammy, of course, and the international sales defied all expectations. It was probably the very last moment you could make money like that off a recording – just at the instant the recorded music market was going down the tubes. Even Djeli's had to reconceptualize the business end of things since then. Who would have thought he'd be talking with Sony about ringtones?

But he doesn't like to get lost in that kind of thing. The real reconceptualization after *À Tierno Bokar* was musical. Not that Djeli was dissatisfied, but his curiosity is insatiable. He's constantly researching, incorporating change. He doesn't tell me a lot about how his new songs are developing. But I get little hints from our correspondence about some of the things that might turn up in his lyrics. Since we communicate about so much – the books we're reading, the films we've seen, little anecdotes from our daily lives – I naturally wonder sometimes if some of this will be reflected in the songs he's writing. He let me listen to the master of *Peau* a few weeks before it was released late last year. It was on his laptop, and I had to hear it on headphones. We'd just had sex. As I told you, when we see each other we generally need to get that out of our systems before we can talk about anything else. So the circumstances were not ideal. He was lying back on the pillows looking very calm, watching me hearing this for the first time.

Now I can tell you, I think *Peau* is in many ways superior even to *À Tierno Bokar*. Texturally, it's exquisitely pared-down. The lyrics are extremely spare. There's very little Bambara, and my French is pretty good, so I was able to follow almost everything. But, I hate to admit, I had a hard time listening to it with any objective distance that first time. I couldn't help straining to hear a trace of myself in the lyrics. This little hunt-and-search operation made it hard to hear the deceptively simple elegance of the music. I was distracted by the multiple references to sex, which sounded discouragingly like reminiscences of other bodies than my own. That "beautiful, dumb Thai girl" made a pretty obvious appearance (not, of course, in these words), as did a few other probably both real and imagined breasts, loins, fingers, and necks, none of which evoked my own person. Except for one thing: I'm not sure, but I suspect the brief, tender, clever, and suspended image of the "*paupière de chagrin*" might have been a reference to my lazy right eyelid which had seemed to fascinate him so that time in bed.

Friday, May 27, 2005, 0:37 a.m.
Subject: Je mets ma main sur ton genou.

I loved Pierrot le fou completely. How funny I hadn't seen it before. It had everything to do with everything. Of course I always loved À bout de souffle because who wouldn't, and Le Mépris affected me profoundly. And I watched Masculin féminin with Sandro, who loves Jean-Pierre Léaud and wanted to see everything with him after he saw Les 400 coups. And we saw Weekend, which is also great. But Pierrot le fou I loved in many ways. I loved her singing, and the slapstick, and the discontinuous music and the paintings and comic strips.

And do you remember – there's Coca-Cola and violence! The dwarf is drinking a bottle of it just before she nails him in the back of the neck with the scissors.

I watched it alone. Sandro went camping with his class from school. I'll watch it again with him when he gets back. I know he'll love it.

I wrote an article about Charlie Parker and photography. I think it might interest you.

Florence is also traveling. She went on a cruise to Alaska with her parents and her brother. She sends me funny descriptions of the weirdos she meets on the boat, and in the bars in the ports of Alaska.

When you read this I guess you'll be back in Paris. I hope you're well. I'm a little lonely without Sandro but sometimes it's good to be alone.

After I'd sent the sestina, Djeli asked why I'd placed the hotel in the neighborhood of Neve Tzedek (he didn't know where that was) instead of the Quartier du Fleuve, which he thought, rightly, was a beautiful name. I thought it was funny that he didn't understand why I might want to protect his privacy. And protect myself from Mariam. He liked the fact that I'd described the scene as "cinematic." In the exchanges that followed, we began discussing film, and as you can see, he recommended *Pierrot le fou*. We agree about a lot of films, but we disagree about a few. I like Wang Kar-Wai. He doesn't, particularly, although he conceded to being moved by *Happy Together* when he first saw it. He said he couldn't remember a lot of details, but that it had struck him as having "a thin membrane. Bruised."

You see what I mean about his delicate sensibility.

Sembène had even pushed him to think about filmmaking himself, but I think he knows his real gifts are elsewhere. That is, he toyed with the idea, but when Sembène passed away last year I think that dream also died. It's not as though he doesn't already have enough on his plate. In the last couple of months, for example, he had a benefit concert for Cité Soleil with his best friend, Wyclef Jean. He also did a benefit performance at the New Orleans Jazz Festival. He was briefly back in Bamako for a private strategy meeting with Amadou Toumani Touré, the president. He spoke at the third World Congress Against the Death Penalty at the Cité universitaire internationale de Paris. He attended, though didn't speak at, the Conference on Moral Particularism at Paris I. There's a documentary filmmaker who's been following him around with a small crew. That's been going on since last September. Djeli goes back and forth between finding him entertaining and a pain in the ass. And of course, there's the regular media attention. This seems to flair up when he indulges himself in dinner dates with supermodels. When the pictures turn up in the tabloids, Mariam freaks out and everybody's rattled for a couple of weeks. When I raise an eyebrow about this kind of thing, he looks at me like a naughty kid and says, "It's not my fault, they keep calling me!" The supermodels, he means.

So what is it, you're thinking, that a man like Djeli sees in me? I'm ten years older, I don't inhabit that world of glamour, I don't even have much patience for it. But I satisfy Djeli's other desires – intellectual, and poetic. Even though the only recorded trace I've found of myself in his artistic output was that paper-thin eyelid of regret, I really do think our correspondence feeds his process. In fact, he just wrote me to say that he might use that image of a castrato *"jouant au* mini golf*"* in a song inspired by Cage. He'd never be so base as to steal one of my own good turns of phrase, but I think my general linguistic sensibility in English has had an effect on his. Once, when we hadn't seen each other for a while, and I was also feeling kind of overwhelmed by my love for Sandro, I wrote him, "Sometimes the heart is hungry like a stomach and you're not sure exactly what you want. That's a good line, isn't it?" He wrote back that yes, it was a good line.

As a form of research for writing this book, I've been reading a few things – as I mentioned in that e-mail to the paramour the other day – travel books, the collected writings of El Sup (he also co-authored a mystery novel! I'm halfway through it), and *The Mandarins*. Then, as luck would have it, I found a remainder of *A Transatlantic Love Affair* in Mercer Street Books. This is Simone de Beauvoir's side of her correspondence with Algren. Her adopted daughter published these letters after Simone's death, and her introduction suggests that she was fulfilling Simone's wish, although she said she'd have liked the chance to clean up her own errors. Sylvie Le Bon de Beauvoir left the errors in, not (if you take her at her word) out of spite, but because she wanted to show how the correspondence affected Simone's written English over time. She starts out making some kind of silly errors, but her prose gets increasingly sophisticated.

Sylvie couldn't include Algren's side of the correspondence, even though she had physical possession of his letters, which her mother had saved. Apparently there was some conflict with his estate about copyright. She paraphrases a few things he wrote in editorial notes, just so Simone's references will make sense.

Well, never mind my comparison of our correspondence to that of Simone de Beauvoir and Nelson Algren. Simone was incredibly demonstrative! Within days of meeting Algren, she was gushing about her undying love. So much for saying "I love you" being a peculiarly "American" trait. Or maybe she was trying to find an "American" writing voice and she thought this was it. Sylvie really hammers home how foreign they were to one another. She says it was like they were from different planets. She refers to the liberating effects of the "unanticipated arrival of this boor, this alien being" into Simone's world. Actually, it was Simone who landed first in his world, but never mind. I like thinking of myself as a "boor." In that respect, anyway, the parallel may hold.

We were eating kedjenou, stewed chicken with peppers, at the African Grill in Bamako when Mariam appeared, tall and luminous in a pale blue boubou. Her head-tie had come off and her hair was mussed. I thought her shining black eyes would burn holes in me. I'd never seen somebody in that much pain. That's when she dumped the Coke on my head.

Djeli met Mariam when he was still a student. It was actually she who had the ambition to make it as a singer in Paris. She encouraged Djeli to perform, and when he started to get a following, she was his back-up singer. She performed with him through her pregnancy with Issa in 1996, but after he was born she decided to shift her energies to the business side of things. Four years later they had Farka. The kids were 8 and 4 when things fell apart. At first, she took the boys to Bamako, which was hard for them. Djeli and Mariam had bought some property there, but they rarely went back. But Mariam felt isolated now in Paris and wanted to be near her family. Djeli told me later how much he suffered during that period, missing his kids. He's an extremely dedicated father. Now, depending on Mariam's moods, they sometimes come to stay with him in Paris. When they come, their nurse comes with them. The kids are beautiful. When I visit and they're there, I feel a little shy around them. Djeli tries to get them to speak English with me, but Issa calls it "*cette langue affreuse.*" I don't take this personally. I try to make do with my fumbling French. They seem neutral. I can't blame them.

Monday, December 5, 2005, 1:23 a.m.
Subject: It took me a couple of days to recover but now I'm okay

You have that beautiful expression in French – "l'amitié amoureuse". I think that's what we have – at least it's what I feel for you. In the middle of your kind of confused speech about the "fragmentation of your affective life," I wasn't sure if you still thought it would be possible to maintain this friendship. Which has been very precious to me. I thought, "Who else is going to describe a film to me as having 'a thin membrane, bruised'?"

I think you're one of the great poets of our time. One of the five most intelligent men I've ever met in my life. I think that sometimes you say idiotic things. I think you need to learn to let the other person lead in bed. I have a lot of affection for you.

It's funny, although he's very graceful, any time Djeli and I have attempted couples dancing he's had a profound disinclination to lead, but in sex he tends to take a very traditional masculine role. He's surprisingly uncomfortable letting someone else take over. He doesn't really like fellatio. He even stooped to invoke national stereotypes in regard to his distaste for the blow-job. *"Bon,"* he said, *"tu es américaine…"* as though that explained anything. When I said I thought that had little to do with this, he relented. This message about *"l'amitié amoureuse,"* of course, followed one of our early visits. He'd been very warm, almost effusive in his affections. We stayed up late after sex talking about film, politics, music, and books. One night we were lying in bed together. There was a pause in the conversation. I kissed his shoulder. Djeli smelled faintly of coconut oil. He drew my head upward, brushed the hair from my eyes and said, "I want to play something for you." We were both naked. He got his kora from the corner and propped himself up at the head of the bed and began to play.

Imagine being the unique and privileged listener to the most beautiful music in the world. He began to sing, softly, in that haunting falsetto of his. It was an old song, traditional, one of the first his father had taught him. A tear rolled down his cheek as he sang. Afterwards, he wiped away the tear and said that sometimes he cried like this when he played for his sons. He said he was moved because he knew I was hearing this beautiful song for the first time.

But just at the end of my stay in Paris, he seemed to pull back. There was that awkward conversation about "fragmentation." Things were complicated with Mariam. There were obviously some other women he'd seen. That didn't worry me particularly. I was just afraid of losing the correspondence. I would be very sad to lose the correspondence.

But pretty quickly he warmed up again. One day he wrote to say that he missed me and he wanted to see me in New York. He said he thought we needed to "talk." Then I felt safe enough to be honest about my feelings, without actually using the word "love."

Friday, February 3, 2006, 8:37 a.m.
Subject: how I woke up

My alarm clock is the kind that plays CDs. This week I put in Jouissance. I woke up every morning hearing you singing "Quiconque." It's so beautiful, that song.

I think of you often, sometimes with affection, sometimes with desire, sometimes with awe. Sometimes all at once.

CHAPTER 2: THE PURLOINED LETTER

Wednesday, January 23, 2008, 0:42 a.m.
Subject: fort/da

I forgot to thank you for the list of my "advantages," for saying that I'm smart and my body is beautiful. Thank you. But when I said you should love me, that wasn't why. You should love me for my peculiarities – for being strange, as I love your strangeness. You're very strange.

I didn't write anything about the Todd Haynes film, or that article in the NLR, or Pablo's party, or the cigars, or Kurt Weill. Stop playing this annoying game of fort/da!

I spent part of January with the paramour. I think this was the closest we've been. We were together for a week, almost all the time. But as soon as I got back to New York, I got another one of those "I love you but I'm not in love with you" messages. It was really irritating. We'd already been through this before. My lover generously appended a list of reasons I would make an excellent life partner, and yet despite all these "advantages," it seems that doubt lingered. I was a little too polite to point out all the potential disadvantages, from my own perspective, of our being together: Hannah's understandable and yet still fairly terrifying volatility; the wrath of the ETA *and* Homeland Security; the smirking disdain of the youthful, media-crazed art world; and the seemingly endless parade of leggy supermodels. Oh, and there was also the little inconvenience that we lived on different continents.

When Santutxo got my abbreviated response, he wrote back asking what "fort/da" meant. I would have thought he'd have heard about this from his shrink.

Don't tell me it surprises you that the paramour sees a Lacanian psychoanalyst.

Forgive me if you find this basic knowledge, but given that it had slipped even the memory of my erudite friend, maybe I should remind you: Freud tells the story in *Beyond the Pleasure Principle* of a little boy who's always throwing his toys into the corner and under the bed. He's a nice kid but this habit is a little inconvenient. Then one day Freud watches him playing with a spool. The kid tosses it away and shouts, "*fort!*" which means "gone!" Then he reels the spool back and says, "*da!*" which means "there!" And Freud figures out that this is repetition compulsion: the kid is rehearsing the big thing he's learned to do, which is to separate from his mother.

So, you see, my message to Santutxo was not particularly subtle. It was kind of Freud with a mallet. When I reminded him of the story, he seemed vaguely disgruntled, but he said he got it. It was, I must confess, a pretty self-congratulatory interpretation of his pattern of pulling me close and then pushing me away. At the time, I basically believed that this was true – that he was compulsively rehearsing our separations so he could imagine himself to be in control of them. Of course I figured these separations were also replaying some trauma that well pre-dated me. But at this point I'm starting to take his rejections a little more seriously. I think they may be personal.

I don't know if he took this up with his analyst. I suspect not. I have a funny feeling he's pretty selective about what he tells his shrink. And you know, appointments with Lacanians are famously short. I'd love for her to read this manuscript. But obviously, that would tell her a lot more about my own neuroses than Santutxo's.

She's already got her hands full with him. When I wrote,

"You're very strange," I wasn't exaggerating. Of course, what would you expect? Pick your primal scene. He's seen a lot of things nobody should see. His father's bloodied mug with a black hole where his teeth used to be. Melitón's fish eyes staring back accusingly out of his dead head. His own bruised, charred, punctured, zapped, and slashed limbs, first at the hands of GAL, and later the ETA. Luz's bandaged stump. Here's a shocker: Santutxo's afraid of dying.

You know, Jacques Lacan had a very interesting way of explaining the repetition compulsion, and I've been thinking about it in relation to the e-mail that got trapped in my spam filter, and some other glitches we've encountered in our correspondence. I'm referring to the famous "Seminar on 'The Purloined Letter.'" In this essay, Lacan analyzes a story by Edgar Allan Poe. In the story, which is narrated by an unnamed friend of the private investigator, Dupin, who unravels the mystery, the Queen is nearly caught reading a clandestine letter from her lover. The King walks in and she decides that the best way to hide it is to leave it lying, face down, right out in the open. The King is a little slow so this goes right past him. But the tricky Minister walks in, and he sees right away what's up. So he nonchalantly lays a similar looking letter right next to the Queen's, then coughs or makes some other distracting noise, I don't remember exactly, and picks up the incriminating document and walks out. He holds onto this letter for a long time, and uses it to harass and politically intimidate the Queen. She gets the cops to search his house when he's not there, and they look in all the most crafty, secret places, to no avail. That's when they call in this Dupin character, who's interested in the reward, but also harbors some resentment toward the Minister. He goes for an ostensibly friendly visit, and right away figures out that the Minister is playing the Queen's game: the letter's right out in the open, just a little crumpled and refolded with a new address. So Dupin returns the next day, producing a crumpled letter of his own. He creates some distraction, and does the Minister's switcheroo. Dupin leaves a humiliating little message on his decoy letter for the evil Minister. He gets the reward, and the Queen gets her letter back.

Lacan points out that the Minister is compulsively repeating the Queen's action. His interpretation of this is fairly complicated. It has to do with the way in which the subject is constituted by the symbolic order. Really, it doesn't matter who fills that role – somebody has to. The implications are fairly distressing. You think you're writing your own plot, but you're really just getting plugged into a signifying chain. And Lacan asks, "And is it not such effects which justify our referring, without malice, to a number of imaginary heroes as real characters?"

Hello, Santutxo.

Lacan ends the seminar with the famous and perplexing statement, "a letter always arrives at its destination." A lot of people have weighed in about what this means. It's obviously nothing so simple as saying the Queen got her letter back and things always go this smoothly. Most people think it means that when we get plugged into that signifying chain, it doesn't really matter if we're in the "wrong" place – we're just playing out our neurotic destiny. Jacques Derrida took issue with that last line, though. He liked the idea of the possibility of letters getting lost in the mail. That is, language that would get detached from a singular, true "meaning." But Slavoj Žižek said Derrida didn't get the point: it wasn't that all letters got where they were "supposed" to go. He said a message in a bottle arrives at its destination the moment it's thrown into the sea.

Tuesday, May 17, 2005, 10:56 a.m.
Subject: message in a bottle

I'm sorry that you lost two messages that you wrote to me,
but I kind of like the idea of them having existed without my
having read them. I think this is part of what I like about e-
mail. It feels like a message in a bottle that might get swal-
lowed up in the ether. It's so abstract.

That was a message from very early in our correspondence.
Obviously, there had been some problem with Santutxo's server.
He said he'd composed two long and carefully drafted messages
but somehow they got lost before he could send them. That had
also happened to me before. As I said in my message, I kind of
like that about e-mail.

I'm having a flashback to that dinner party in New York,
when Slavoj Žižek and Gayatri Spivak were standing there politely chewing on my edible flowers while Analia Hounie poured
Santutxo a Coke.

When I got the very first e-mail from Santutxo, I wasn't
sure I could believe it was from him. One of the things that
seemed weird was that he had a Yahoo! account. On the other hand, what should I have expected? His own address at
arranobeltza.com? Obviously I can't publish his e-mail address,
but it's a kind of lame joke involving one of his aliases. Because
he opens up the Yahoo! page to check his e-mail, he often reads
the Yahoo! news. Every time he mentions something he's read
there, he refers to it as Yahoo!, with the exclamation point. You
can see why this all seems kind of funny, coming from an iconic
revolutionary figure. He seems to take seriously the news flashes

he reads on the Yahoo! homepage. Sometimes they'll prompt him to ask me for an update on political events unfolding here. He also displays a surprising curiosity about pop culture items. He says that Cameron Diaz seems like an interesting person.

So in a way, it would seem that Santutxo's use of the internet for personal correspondence and general websurfing is like the average person's. But every once in a while, one or the other of us gets a little paranoid about who might be looking in. These days, of course, he's not planning any violent actions. Excommunicated from the ETA, even his broadcast political missives are what you might call ex-communiqués. Swerving unpredictably from the radical to the reactionary, nobody actually thinks they'll come to any material end.

But it wasn't always like this. He spent the '70s practically running the ETA show from Mexico City. A lot of people would take issue with this account, and of course there was only so much he could help with in terms of practical strategizing for individual operations. But the Arrano Beltza's broadcasts were the poetic heart and soul of Euskadi Ta Askatasuma, simultaneously the clearest and most lyrical expressions of its fundamental political philosophy. I'm talking, of course, about the ETA-PM, the Political-Military Front. Santutxo already had friction with the more militant faction, the ETA-M, but he had this uncanny ability to persuade even some of the most extreme to let go of their bloodiest dreams. He believed in "blood, when necessary," but never civilian.

Still, 1980 was the ETA's bloodiest year since its formation. It was a difficult time for Santutxo. Amets was supportive but she was getting increasingly frustrated by his emotional unavailability. She didn't blame him – she knew it was for a higher cause, but it's hard to love a saint, and Amets needed affection. Aitor was still pretty little, but even then, he seemed to know that as dedicated a father as he was, Santutxo's idealism made him extremely vulnerable. To this day, I think Aitor feels protective of his dad.

Around 1983, the "anti-terrorist" terrorist organization GAL was formed to fight a dirty war against the ETA. Things got really scary. Santutxo knew he had to go back. Amets and Aitor stayed behind. It was terribly sad for everybody, but they knew it had to be this way.

For the next four years, Santutxo was back in the trenches. He didn't carry out any actions himself, of course, but he was now deeply involved in the practical strategizing. He continued sending out communiqués, and you could see that while they still manifested his completely unique combination of lyricism, intelligence, and humor, the Arrano Beltza was starting to crack a little under the pressure.

In 1987, against his passionate objections, the extremist wing of the ETA bombed a supermarket garage in Barcelona. Twenty-four innocent people were killed. Santutxo was devastated. The ETA apologized for the "mistake." There was a particularly sad story about a young girl who had survived the explosion. She was eighteen. She was a ballet dancer. Her left leg had been ripped off by the blast. Disguised as a hospital orderly, Santutxo began visiting her every day. Two years later, Luz was living with him in Donostia, pregnant with Bakar.

We were eating pintxos at Goiz Argi in the Parte Vieja when she appeared out of nowhere: an extravagantly beautiful, agonized woman in her 30s, with green eyes, dark brows, cascading black curls, and a prosthetic leg, screaming in Castilian that I was not the aging plain-Jane journalist that she'd been led to believe. And then came the Coke, and the violence.

I've been reading those letters from Simone de Beauvoir to Nelson Algren. In late November of 1947, it seems there was a postal strike in France. Their correspondence was interrupted both ways. She found this very distressing. She sent him a telegram saying, "STRIKE STOPS LETTERS NOT MY HEART WAIT PATIENTLY WARMEST LOVE   SIMONE." She kept writing, despite the clogged communication pipeline, and he did too. Eventually they got the backed up letters. It seems that during the hiatus, he wrote her about some other women he'd considered sleeping with. She refers to them as "the phoney blonde," "the Jewish girl," and "the older woman." She says that she is dead set against sexual jealousy, though she can't help but feel it a little. Still, she encourages him to go ahead and indulge his desires – just to be sure to kick anybody out of the Chicago apartment when she gets back to town.

She also talks about the people in Paris who are trying to seduce her: an "ugly lesbian," another "Jewish girl," and a velvety creep named "Puma." She indicates that she's also open to sleeping around. She seems to take some pleasure in cataloging their respective potential strange bedfellows.

Speaking of strange bedfellows, but in the figurative sense of the term, you might be interested in another of Santutxo's complicated friendships – that with Baltasar Garzón Real. Garzón, perhaps you know, is often referred to as Spain's "*Juez Estrella*" – the Rock Star Judge. He had a famous and pyrotechnic debate in 2003 with El Sup over the Basque question. Garzón's persecution of alleged ETA operatives has been, you might say, rabid. He's done pretty much anything he could do to eviscerate the movement, shutting down legitimate news outlets on the grounds of "terrorist" ties, intimidating community activists, and basically being a pain in every Basque ass. So what the hell, you may ask, is Santutxo doing cozying up to him? I have to say, I do have my own doubts about Garzón, but he's nearly as complicated a case as Santutxo. He was the one who issued that arrest warrant in 1998 for Pinochet, for the torture and murder of Spanish citizens in Chile. He started a flood of suits over the disappearance of Spaniards in Argentina's dirty war. He went after Kissinger over Operation Condor. More recently, he tried to get a European block to suspend Berlusconi's immunity. And around the time he was having that row with El Sup, he was simultaneously blasting the US over human rights abuses in Guantánamo Bay and the Iraq war. I have to say, while he can be something of a blow-hard, I was pretty charmed by his public threat last year to sue Bush for catastrophic imbecility.

As you can imagine, Garzón has had to keep his friendship with Santutxo under wraps. The press – from both the left and right – would have a field day if they got their hands on this. But El Sup knows, and of course Garzón is fully aware of Santutxo's history with Marcos. Frankly, I think they're both a little jealous.

Monday, August 14, 2006, 11:22 a.m.
Subject: Lebanon

I've been thinking about your posture in relation to Lebanon, and Garzón's reaction, and mine. It's strange, that first night that we saw each other, you touched on the subject right away. I thought it was a little weird, but I didn't feel like debating with you, and I wasn't even really – I think – too disturbed, because in that moment, I could even kind of see your logic (without agreeing), but I knew that as an American I couldn't ever assume that posture, it would be hateful in an American, but in you, somehow it wasn't exactly – it was complicated, but it wasn't frightening, because you from your position kind of have to assume a contrary position, in order to maintain some perspective on the complexity of the situation. But it's not easy to hear. And then afterwards you described Garzón's suffering – I thought it was beautiful that you saw he was suffering, and that you understood why he was feeling that, because he must love you a lot, and these things hurt – I asked myself if that little sadness of mine had anything to do with this also. But I don't think so. I think it was that other thing. But since you were talking about Bush's religiosity, everything became confused – politics, personal pain, everything.

Here's something funny: when Sandro woke up on Saturday morning, he said, "I had a nightmare. I was chasing two guys on a motorcycle, shouting revolutionary phrases. The two guys were pro-Bush. They were holding their fists in the air and shouting, 'Go Bush!' The strange thing was, they looked totally left wing. One of them was a Rasta."

Santutxo liked this dream. He generally likes the things Sandro says, even though he finds him too predictably "politically correct." One time I asked Sandro if he thought that he and I were hippies. This was in reference to that "antipathetic" comment I'd made in an article regarding Santutxo's hippie image in the 1970s. Sandro thought about it for a while, and then he said, no, that he thought a better description of the two of us would be "clean philosophers with disturbing tendencies." When I told Santutxo about this, he said he wanted to join our club.

But I began this chapter with a reference to misdirected mail, and I guess it's time for me to tell you about the most significant glitch in our correspondence – the dead letter that almost left me dead as well. You may think I'm exaggerating.

It was only after that "cunt" e-mail went missing that I finally consulted with an IT guy and figured out about the spam filter. I honestly didn't even know I had a filter. I get plenty of spam, and I'd sent and received any number of e-mails with naughty bits in them. The filter seems to be arbitrary, and weirdly selective. That's why the first time this happened, I really didn't have a clue. It never occurred to me that somebody could be sending me important information and it could get caught in that net. The filter, I later learned, traps suspect messages for a period of a week, and then automatically and permanently deletes them. So while I managed to retrieve the "cunt" one before it got sucked away into oblivion, I never did receive the message I'm telling you about now. (You can pause here to think about Lacan, Derrida, and Žižek, or not, as you please.)

It was during a period when Santutxo had begun to suspect that he was being followed again. He wasn't sure by whom. Garzón swore he knew nothing about the government's involvement, and the ETA hadn't seemed to be paying too much attention recently. Still, there were some disturbing signs: objects on his desk that appeared to have been tampered with, a cigarette butt left mysteriously in his toilet, a creepy guy who was hanging out a lot across the street. He mentioned these things to me, but I told you, Santutxo's neurotic. He also mentioned a lot of medical "symptoms" that sounded pretty benign to me.

We were making plans for a visit. Even though I thought he was exaggerating the risk, I decided to give in to his suggestion that we meet this time not at his place in Donostia, but at a safe house about an hour out of town. It was a farmhouse owned by a friend of a friend – obviously, I'm not at liberty to disclose much more than that. Let's just say it was yet another "strange bedfellow."

When my plane landed in Barcelona, I checked my Black-Berry for messages. There was a bit of spusa-listserv spam, something vaguely irritating from my editor, and two short messages from Florence asking me about when she should check in on Sandro and if I were wearing the black thigh-high stockings she'd given me to my tryst at the farmhouse (Florence is the soul of discretion). Nothing from Santutxo. Everything appeared to be on track.

I found a driver willing to take me out to the safe house. Of course, I didn't call it that. He seemed a little surprised that somebody like me would be headed in that direction, but a fare's a fare. I swung my satchel into the back seat and we were off. When we got to the farmhouse he asked me if I wanted him to see me to the door. It was already starting to get dark, and this was, as you can imagine, a pretty remote location. I knew Santutxo was feeling paranoid, so I said no and then stood there by the road waving, gesturing to him that it was okay to go. Finally he drove off.

Little sticks crunched under my feet as I made my way to the farmhouse. It was chilly out. The door was slightly ajar and there was a dim light emanating from within. I pushed it with my fingertips. My heart was beating pretty hard. I couldn't wait to have Santutxo's swollen cock pressed up against my body once again. But before I knew what had happened, a scabrous guy with a shaved head and a pierced lip was wrenching both my arms behind my back, breathing into my neck, and an enormous red-haired woman with a mohawk was sneering at me in derision, calling me, mockingly, the Txotxolo's little *"andragai"* (girlfriend). She had a pistol. I thought I could even smell it.

As I said, I never saw the message that Santutxo had sent. But later he told me the content, and a little about the specific turn of phrase that may have activated the despamming mechanism. Just before he left to ready the safe house for my arrival, he got a tip that there would be trouble. He immediately booked me a room in a Barcelona dive hotel, and then wrote to tell me NOT to make the trip out to the country. He relayed the name and location of the hotel, and told me to stay there until he sent further word. His message ended: "And even if I can't be stroking your pussy tonight in ---- as we planned, I'll figure out a way to get to your hotel in Barcelona. I am getting a very hard wood just thinking about it."

I had recently taught Santutxo the English expression "morning wood," which he found very charming and poetic. I told him we also said, somewhat less poetically, "woody" to refer to any masculine erection. He seemed to have confused the terms. I don't think, however, it was Santutxo's erection which set off the spam filter. I think it was my pussy.

* * *

Maybe you find it odd that both the ETA extremists and a public figure as important as Baltasar Garzón Real would pay so much attention to a fictional character like the Arrano Beltza. But this kind of thing has happened before. Djeli once told me a story about the great Kenyan writer Ngũgĩ wa Thiong'o. In 1986 he published a novel in Gikuyu called *Matigari*. It was unusual for an African novel to be published in a non-colonial language, so the people were all talking about it. In fact, they were talking so much about the main character that the government became convinced that he was a real person and issued a warrant for his arrest.

And then there's the reverse process, which I guess happens a little more frequently. El Sup, for example, wrote himself into that mystery novel.

Obviously, these kinds of questions interest me, because, as I mentioned, I occasionally dick around writing fiction. Look, I'm dicking around right now. That's a rather vulgar way to put it but as you'll remember, the paramour likes the word "dick," and every once in a while I find myself using it, and various other salty American expressions. The paramour, after all, is kind of my ideal reader, so I do what I can to be entertaining. In spite of the demands of greatness, my lover has generously reviewed and commented on various failed efforts, claiming to find me a writer of some charm. When pressured, Sandro will also look things over, and Florence can be counted on in a pinch. I can also turn to my mother, though sometimes I hesitate on account of questions of seemliness. I'm sure you see what I mean. But for the last three years, the paramour has generally been the first set of editorial eyes.

Binh and I had a pretty interesting exchange going on for a while there about the significance of plot in a novel. When it comes to literary terminology, Binh tends to use French. In my early efforts, he noted that I appeared to be a *romancière sans intrigue*. He was being a little cheeky. You know, *intrigue* is French for *plot*, but he knew (and pointed out) that because the French term for *novelist* sounded to Anglophone ears like a romance-artist, this would make me sound not like a plotless novelist, but like a really dull lover. Of course, he insisted that contrary to appearances, my plotlessness was actually very arousing. He found my theoretical digressions "sexy."

Binh's little play on words may have been cheeky, but really, he had a very touching reaction to the manuscripts I'd sent him. I wrote to thank him for his comments, and I answered his etymological questions about the English term *plot*.

Thursday, August 31, 2006, 2:41 p.m.

Subject: intrigue

Plot - comes from the Middle English, and the first meaning is a parcelle de terrain, a plot of land. Then a map of that terrain. And from map comes the plan or outline of a story. But it's also a verb meaning to connive. It has nefarious connotations. You plot to kill the king.

You see? You preferred my first manuscript, which was a roman sans intrigue. Moi aussi, je préfère les romans sans intrigue. I always said I couldn't write anything with a plot. Only poems, or essays. But after I wrote a novel without a plot, everyone (everyone but you) said "where's the plot?" So I tried to write a novel with a plot. And everyone else said, "I like the plot but what's with all those long weird digressions?" And you said, "I like the long weird digressions but I have a problem with the fictional part." You're so strange. I love the way you read me.

I think we'll never agree about racial representations. In this respect, I'm American. It's generational, too. I know that. I also know my country is full of hypocrisy about these things. I see that. Still, I found some of the images in your new series very objectifying. Of course that happens here all the time, but in advertising. The exploitation is explicit. And I still find it strange when you refer to your "petite africaine." I realize nobody escapes ethnic eroticism. We already had that long exchange. Hiroshima, mon amour. All of that. But it's complicated. And Americans will always hear it differently.

All my pictures of flowers come from my little digital camera, but the bonobos came from Google. If you type "bonobo sex" in Google images you will be surprised what pops up. And though I've tried my best not to be vulgar, I'm sending you a SHOCKING image of une femelle à se masturber. Because I thought she was beautiful.

Please excuse me if you find this message enervating. I told you once, even when I disagree with you, I find you fascinating, and very moving.

I send you a kiss.

You see how things run together in our correspondence. I was talking about the etymology of "plot" and suddenly we were in the terrain of race and eroticism. But of course we were also already in the terrain of romance and intrigue, so maybe it's not such a leap. The part about the bonobos I'll explain later.

The long and the short of it is: Binh has a strange and wonderful sensibility which sometimes disturbs me, but always intrigues me. And he seems to feel this way about me. This may explain our repetition compulsion. Which is to say, we often seem to be coming back to the same conversation. I'm talking about me and Binh, but I could of course be talking about Tzipi.

Why do we both persist in having multiple lovers? It's not that we're squeamish about commitment. I told you, the paramour is fundamentally a monogamist. I know I also have that impulse. I think the most plausible explanation is Lacan's. When he's analyzing "The Purloined Letter," he anticipates the question of why it's the Minister who compulsively repeats the Queen's bad action: "The plurality of subjects, of course, can be no objection for those who are long accustomed to the perspectives summarized by our formula: *the unconscious is the discourse of the Other*…" I know you may find this unsettling, but the truth is, it doesn't *matter* that it's somebody else. It's *always* somebody else.

I already mentioned that e-mail I wrote with the subject heading "fiction" – the one about "falling in love" and the impossibility of believing in the paramour's singular necessity. I attributed that to "emotional distance," and I said that there were all those other kinds of distance between us – of language, nation, age, social context. Fame. But of course later Binh and I got to discussing whether eros even exists without *some* kind of difference – even between lovers of the same sex. The other question is whether eros ever exists without similarity.

Binh is extremely sensitive to language, but he also has access to this other language – the language of light and color and shape – and often his most poetic messages are videos, or just embedded images – take, for example, this photograph of his nipple, staring back at the camera like a pure, unblinking eye:

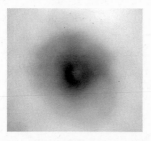

I treasure these communications. It's not just that they tend to be so erotically potent. They're often full of wit, or tenderness, or fear, or pain.

But because I tend to write more words, he sometimes expresses a kind of intimidation about our correspondence.

Sunday, April 1, 2007, 1:02 a.m.
Subject: words

"Désembarrassée" is the generous version. Another way of saying I have logorrhea. I write too much. I'm the one who gets completely inarticulate talking to you. Especially after sex, when you suddenly begin to speak with what our friend Holland Cotter referred to as your "almost devastating elegance."

Speaking of sex, I woke up again wanting you. I touched my whole body and came with two fingers inside myself. It was slippery and muscular and beautiful, and I was imagining what you would be feeling if my fingers were your sex.

I was referring, of course, to that enormous, adoring piece Cotter had written in the *Times* about Binh's Guggenheim show. I agreed with everything he said. I'm often devastated by that elegance. And I often wake up like this, wanting Binh.

He liked that paragraph about my fingers. He later told me it made him remember exactly what it felt like when his sex was in mine. He sent me back a .mov file. At first, I was a little confused when I saw it on that little QuickTime viewer. It seemed to be a snail, or a slug – some strange mauve creature, but with a delicate, powdery texture. Whatever it was, it was moving slowly, struggling, lifting its heavy head. Its unhurried, narcotic motion was mesmerizing. There was a kind of halo around it. It shifted, and began to grow. And as it grew, I realized with a smile what it was. It was Binh's unspeakably beautiful, perfect, uncircumcised penis rising up in a graceful erection.

It swayed there on my computer screen, tumescent, magnificent creature, with that strange, golden halo around it. I almost put my mouth on the screen.

Given our age difference, it will not surprise you to learn that one issue that repeatedly comes up in Binh's sessions with his shrink is his relationship with his mother. I told you, the paramour only fell in love once, in childhood. Despite his utter dedication to her, Binh rarely calls his mother on the phone. She's resistant to e-mail, but even if she weren't, I'm not sure Binh would write her. She, like me, has also complained of his lack of demonstrativeness. Some art critic once did a story on Binh's early life in Hanoi, and when he interviewed his mother, she smiled and shook her head, saying, "Binh was always very distant." She adores him as much as he her, but they both seem to acknowledge the necessity of the distance, both geographical and psychological, that Binh has had to place between them.

I still haven't met her. And since things seem to be petering out, I guess maybe I never will. It would be awkward, anyway. She's still having a hard time getting over the fact that Binh separated from Aafke. She thinks a man's place is with his family. Binh's father died years ago, but when he was alive, he was a very good husband. Binh says his parents were in love until the day his father died. He really thought he'd be with Aafke to the end as well. But it wouldn't take a psychoanalyst to figure out that they didn't begin under the most auspicious of circumstances. They were both just kids. It all happened so fast.

When Binh was seventeen, he was one of five students selected from the Hanoi University of Fine Arts to travel to Paris 8 under the auspices of an exchange sponsored by the French government. Three of the others were painters. One was a sculptor. Binh was the only "conceptual" artist of the bunch. He was also the youngest, the smartest, the most freakishly gifted, and the most promiscuous. In Paris, he was like a kid in a candy store. He went to underground performance art events in the scuzziest warehouses of the *banlieue*. He went to smoky experimental video screenings in the swank apartments of art school *ingénues*. He made out with boys and girls. Everybody wanted him. It wasn't just his physical beauty – they could sense already his brilliance. It was that "old soul" thing. Binh is very special.

He met Aafke in a café where she was waiting tables – a luminous Dutch girl with cornflower blue eyes and hair the color of butter. He told her it was funny to find himself with a Dutch girl because when he was a kid he used to joke that he was a Swede. He meant, of course, that his political impulses put him out of sync with most Vietnamese. He had a particular abhorrence of anything that whiffed of sexism. From a very tender age, Binh declared himself a feminist.

When they first started going out, Binh told me, Aafke had seemed to correspond to his sexual open-mindedness. She had adventures of her own. Sometimes they had them together. Binh said, "In the beginning, she was so EU." Everybody was invited. But when they decided to get married she started to get more territorial – especially after she became pregnant with Bao and Bob. Twins. I've seen them several times when they've come to stay with Binh. He's an extremely dedicated father. You can't imagine how beautiful they are: glowing copper-colored skin, copper-colored hair, copper eyes. It's as though Binh had spent hours enhancing their digital tone, hue, and saturation on his computer.

Aafke had to deliver them by C-section. I'm sure if they had been born in the US the hospital wouldn't have allowed this, but Binh made a digital video of their birth. He showed me some of the images: close-ups of Aafke's incredibly pale face, the thin blue veins visible under her closed eyelids; the saturated red of her blood as the knife sliced into her abdomen; the two gelatinous, gory, squirming boys wriggling out of the slit. I found the video extremely beautiful, but I understood why even Binh found this material too intimate to use in a public art project. This made me feel a little bit better about the fact that he'd never actually used any images of me, outside of our private correspondence. He didn't seem to mind using images of his other lovers, like that big, pretty Ethiopian girl, or that break-dancer named Jean-Philippe.

Shortly after the twins were born, Binh and Aafke decided to move to Berlin because it was cheaper, and because the experimental art scene struck Binh as more vital. He hooked up with Lars and some other crackpots, Aafke got increasingly pissed off, he couldn't take it anymore, they separated, there was the YouTube thing… and the rest is history.

Saturday, June 9, 2007, 4:08 p.m.
Subject: Darwin

You think you're different (Swedish Vietnamese, homo/heterosexual, right wing leftist, Darwinist feminist…). I also think I'm pretty unusual. Maybe it's a lot of egotism on both our parts. But of course I agree that we are (we should all be) experimental.

Maybe you'll think it's just laziness on my part if I say of some of our differences, "They're generational." Maybe I ought to push him harder on some of these things. Binh may really be a hypocrite. He's certainly been accused of that. His politics are weird. He's constantly assuming the underdog position. He claims, for example, to be fundamentally gay, even though the vast preponderance of his sexual activity is with women. He told me that André Gide liked to say that he was a "*lesbien*," as opposed to a *lesbienne*. I can't even begin to go into the Darwin business right now. Suffice it to say that his feminism might, on occasion, come into question.

The funny thing is, Sandro shares some of these oddball tendencies. And in him, too, I find it all frustrating and yet weirdly hopeful and innocent.

We were planning a visit. We decided to book a room at Propeller Island. Binh suggested the "Two Lions" room. That's probably the kinkiest choice you could make. Here's the description of the room from Lars' website: "Dual cages, situated in the center of this spacious menagerie, rest on stilts measuring 1.5 meters tall and await applause from the neighbouring guests [*Applaus vom Nachbargast*]. Your curtain presides over what your audience sees and what not!"

In preparation for the trip, Florence had purchased me a pair of black thigh-high stockings. I think if it hadn't been his idol, Binh, arranging this tryst, Sandro might have found the whole thing a little theatrical. I did too, to tell the truth, but by the time my plane landed at Tegel I was in a state of almost unbearable sexual excitement. I checked my BlackBerry for messages: a bit of spam, something from my editor, two shorties from Florence – nothing from Binh. I jumped in a cab. At Propeller Island, the girl at the front desk appeared to be very stoned. I asked for the keys to "Two Lions" and she stared at me, wiped her nose on her sleeve, and finally turned them over.

I tapped on the door to see if Binh had gotten there first. He hadn't. I let myself in and tossed my bag on the bed. I thought I'd freshen up. Some of the rooms at Propeller Island don't have their own bathrooms, but this one did. I had to climb up a little tower to get to the throne-like toilet to pee. I climbed back down, undressed, and took a quick shower in the golden tub. I slathered some lotion on, touched up my make-up, and wriggled back into my thigh-highs and a fresh pair of black lace panties. I looked at myself in the mirror. I wasn't sure how much longer I could wait.

I lay on the bed for a while with my eyes closed. It was nearly 11:00 p.m. in Berlin, but of course by New York time it was just late afternoon. I thought about e-mailing Binh but I didn't want to seem overly needy. I figured he'd get there soon.

I found a German copy of Vogue and flipped through it. I texted Sandro reminding him to practice his piano. I lay down some more. I kept checking the BlackBerry.

At 1:15, I scaled the metal ladder into my cage and shut the door. What was I thinking? I was pissed off, I was sad, I was humiliated, I was embarrassed. Part of me was thinking that any minute Binh would turn the key in the lock, let himself in, and find me irresistibly sexy in my ridiculous get-up in the lion cage. Those cages are too small to stand up in. I took two turns crawling around my cage on all fours. Then I flipped over on my back, plunged both hands into my black lace panties, and began masturbating. It took me a surprisingly long time to come, considering I'd been pretty much primed for this since the airplane ride. I think it was because I kept getting distracted wishing Binh would walk in on me.

Still, after I'd finished, I waited just a minute or two and then I started all over again. It was 4 a.m. in Berlin by the time I'd tired myself out.

Binh, meanwhile, was sleeping like a baby in the acoustically muffled "Padded Cell" room about 15 feet away. You see, this was the ending of the message that got caught in my spamtrap: "And even if I won't be stroking your pussy tonight in the lion cage as we planned, I'll be waiting for you just down the hall in the room for crazy people. I am getting a very hard wood just thinking about it."

* * *

Friday, July 28, 2006, 3:12 p.m.
Subject: Why I Am So Wise

All good here. Paris is beautiful. One day it rains, but the next it's sunny. I haven't written much but I've been reading. I brought over Nietzsche's "Why I Am So Wise" for Sandro but he didn't feel like reading it. It's so much fun. Of course the general consensus is that Nietzsche was a misogynist but I find some of the things he says about women kind of charming and totally recognizable, at least in reference to my own person. Look:

"The complete woman perpetrates literature in the same way as she perpetrates a little sin: as an experiment, in passing, looking around to see if someone notices and SO THAT someone may notice..."

Speaking of which, I did finish the lyric for A Zed and Two Noughts. I remembered that your birthday is soon and I decided to give it to you for your birthday. If you get here before we leave I'll give it to you in person but if you don't then I'll send it to you, with the music. It's flawed but in a way I kind of like.

I think of you often here. It's a little irritating.

I wrote this e-mail when Sandro and I were spending two weeks in Paris. I was doing a longish piece on Mathieu Chedid, and since Sandro was on vacation I brought him along. We swapped our apartment in New York with a French couple who lived in the Marais. It was great in many ways. I knew even before I bought the tickets that Djeli would probably be out of town the whole time. He had a show at a festival in Dakar, and then he was going to go to Bamako to visit the kids. There was the slim possibility that he'd come back to Paris before we had to leave.

Staying in Djeli's city without him being there was very

strange. It seemed like everywhere I went there were reminders of him. I'd walk into a restaurant near the Bastille and hear his music playing. There were posters up with his picture, advertising his show at the Zenith in August. I saw an Arab kid on the metro listening to his iPod, mouthing the words to the refrain of *"Semer la zizanie."* As I said, all these reminders were a little irritating.

I'd been thinking I should really write some more poetry. I hadn't done that in a while. Sandro had been playing this piece by Michael Nyman and the melody would stick in my head. I decided to write a lyric for it. I worked on it while Sandro was practicing. There was no piano at the apartment in the Marais, so we'd walk over to a place called Cyberpianos, where you can rent a digital piano with headphones by the hour. I didn't really need to accompany Sandro, but I liked sitting at the little table in this place, reading. It was funny to watch the pianists clacking away at the silent keys, each one in his or her own world. The owner of Cyberpianos was a very nice guy named Michel. He was either gay or pedantically flirtatious. I have a hard time distinguishing with French men. Anyway, he was always complimenting me when we'd go there, saying how young I looked to have a son Sandro's age. One day an old lady came in to look around and when she left she called me *"mademoiselle."* Michel got very excited by that. He said, *"Vous voyez? C'est fantastique, quoi!"*

Anyway, about the *paroles* for "A Zed and Two Noughts": I wrote these at Cyberpianos. When I was halfway through, I realized they were about Djeli. That's when I decided to give them to him for his birthday. They were a little bit sad, and a little bit funny. Djeli said he thought they were extremely beautiful. *"Stupéfiantes."* That was an exaggeration but I was glad he liked them.

I kind of love that quotation from Nietzsche. About how women "perpetrate" literature. Of course it's always reductive to say "women write a certain way," or "men paint with these things in mind," but as I wrote Djeli, I actually recognized myself in that nasty little reduction. Simone de Beauvoir wrote to Nelson Algren about writers she liked and didn't like. She hated women who wrote "like women." Throughout the correspondence she keeps mentioning "the ugly woman who is in love with me" (the editor helpfully identifies her as the writer Violette Leduc, claiming that Leduc referred to herself in precisely this way). They have regular lunch dates at which "the ugly woman" mostly just cries and says how fascinating and attractive Simone is and how this is driving her to suicidal despair. Simone isn't sure why she keeps making these lunch dates. But at one point she does predict that "the ugly woman" will write an excellent novel. She says that this novel will describe a woman's sexuality in a pure, strong, true, and poetic way, as no other book ever has. But a few letters later Simone dismisses "the ugly woman" as really not knowing very much about literature.

Right after that visit in January, when we had seemed to be so close, Djeli had a couple of shows to do in West Africa. A British journalist was going along for the ride. On my way home I wrote Djeli from the airport a pretty heartfelt message about our time together, how close I'd felt to him, and because I was feeling that close, I made the mistake of raising the subject of a couple of moments of seeming miscommunication in our sex. I'm sure you know what I'm talking about – this kind of thing happens to everyone once in a while. Of course it's best just to let these situations pass. The worst idea is probably to touch on it, however tenderly, in an e-mail. While I had felt particularly intimate with him on an emotional level, it hadn't really been the smoothest sailing in bed. Things may have been compounded by the fact that I was menstruating, which wasn't objectionable to either of us, but introduced some minor inconveniences. Dje-li answered with a short and very banal e-mail about the mosquitoes in his hotel room in Ouagadougou. Apparently he'd had to get up in the middle of the night and hunt them down one-by-one. Finally, he conquered them. He sounded kind of pleased with himself.

I shot him back an image I really love, a painting by the DRC painter Chéri Samba called *Lutte contre les moustiques*:

Saturday, January 19, 2008, 8:14 a.m.
Subject: Je te félicite pour ta victoire sur les moustiques.

La lutte continue.

This painting was particularly appropriate, for a couple of reasons. I figured Djeli would understand. In it, the man is saying to his wife, "I'll kill all the leftists. You take care of the ones coming from the right." Obviously, I was referring to Djeli's totally unpredictable political stance. As you know, the paramour resists all doxies. I was also referring to the real mosquitoes. And I just love Chéri Samba.

Djeli didn't respond. That didn't mean much – he often takes a while to get back to me. That could mean anything. Professional obligations, family obligations, general distraction.

Anyway, two days later, I wrote a slightly more extended message:

Monday, January 21, 2008, 4:11 p.m.
Subject: fruit

The week of menstruation is a drag, but in compensation the week of ovulation is a total delight. My sex is like a ripe fruit. Persimmon. Not even I could resist. This made me think of you.

Everything went exactly as I predicted: that little melancholy when I first got back, but when I walked in the door I found Sandro, hilarious, and then Florence came by with a bottle of Malbec and before I knew it I was happy.

Extremely busy. I have two deadlines this week. Tomorrow afternoon I'm flying to Chicago.

And the guy from NME – interesting? Are you already in Bamako? Did you see the kids? Was your triumph over the mosquitoes definitive? I was happy when I got that message because it was so banal. I'd written a kind of sad e-mail, asking about our sex, and you answered about mosquitoes. I told you once, I like hearing about the banal things in your day-to-day life. It makes me feel closer to you.

Okay, I'm going to finish typing up my notes for this article, take a bath, make a little love to myself and go to sleep. I miss you and I hope you're happy.

That was when Djeli responded with that second "I love you but I'm not in love with you" message, the one I said sounded like it was written to himself. It was really unpleasant. And I accused him of playing fort/da. If he didn't take this up with his analyst, he should have. You know, even his mother made that comment about his "distance" in that documentary.

I mention these messages for a couple of reasons: because of the mosquitoes, but also because of this business of a letter which one seems to be writing to someone else, but is really writing to oneself. We all do this, of course. And yet we persist in imagining that a correspondence is a direct communication between two people. And we persist in believing in the singular reality of any given message.

Lacan made some interesting grammatical observations regarding this delusion. He said that in French, you could only speak of a letter – in any sense of the word – with an article attached to it, be it definite or indefinite. For example, he said that you could take something "to the letter" (*à la lettre*), you could receive "a letter" (*une lettre*) at the post office, or you could be a "man of letters" (*avoir des lettres*), but you couldn't say that there was "some letter" (*de la lettre*) anyplace, even if you were referring to lost mail. You would have to refer to *a* lost letter, or *the* lost letter. He explained this in relation to the function of the letter as a signifier. He said that any signifier was the symbol of the absence of the signified – and for this reason had to be unique. "Which is why we cannot say of the purloined letter that, like other objects, it must be *or* not be in a particular place but that unlike them it will be *and* not be where it is, wherever it goes…"

Am I losing you? Think about it this way: even though I "received" the irritating "I love you but I'm not in love with you" message (the banal understanding of "a letter always arrives at its destination"), it's still pretty unclear who was writing what to whom, and who was in any condition to read it when it got there (where?). And as for that message that got caught in my spam filter – it was *and* it was not where it was, wherever it went… Even when it got permanently obliterated by my server.

My writing was interrupted yet again by an incoming message from the paramour. Actually two. There was one relatively chatty one, anecdotal, nothing too significant, which ended with "a kiss" of indeterminate temperature. Since this message was not hot enough to stoke the flames of desire for the romance, it provoked a slightly impertinent response from me. You might even say rude. But funny. I think the tone was disconcerting. I got another short message almost immediately that ended, "Now I go to the shrink." Of course, my lover's sessions with the analyst are regular, but I couldn't help feeling like maybe I'd provoked some discomfort. This felt both bad and good.

The paramour doesn't like to feel out of control. Take, for example, the little exchange Djeli and I had once about oral sex:

Wednesday, October 24, 2007, 6:14 p.m.
Subject: reflexive verbs

I read some Sappho this morning. Do you know the fragment where she's watching a girl that she loves talking to a man? Did I already write you about this? The poem is all askew, because it begins as though it were about him, but she's just displacing herself onto him: "That man is like a god. He's just sitting there talking to you like everything is normal, but me, when I look at you, my mouth is dry, a flame runs under my skin, I start to sweat, I can't talk, I can't see, there's a ringing in my ears, my heart starts to palpitate..." I'm paraphrasing but it's almost just like this.

I loved the connection you made between the reflexive verb and the question of passivity/activity in the reflexive sexual act. I'd already thought about this in other grammatical and sexual circumstances, because the word "passive" is complicated. "Reflexive" too. Look at Sappho.

Thank you for your kisses. I received them all. I would kiss you back in particular places but sometimes you don't like to be kissed there. You said, "fellation is not my cup of tea," which is hilarious because it's such a stuffy way to put it, but also, in English we say "fellatio". Florence once spelled it "fallacio," which was especially funny because it made it look fallacious.

But my kiss would be true.

As I told you, despite the fact that he's in analysis, Djeli had at one point resorted to national stereotypes to explain our differences of opinion about fellatio. He had no resistance to cunnilingus, as you will perhaps have understood from the reference to the location-specific "kisses" he'd sent in the closing of his e-mail to me. I've already disclosed myself as wielding Freud with a pretty heavy hand, so you can take it with a grain of salt when I suggest that Djeli's distaste for "fellation" has anything to do with a fear of losing control in love.

More interesting, perhaps, was that question of reflexivity. Djeli was very interested in hearing about my auto-erotic life. And as you can see, I was never disinclined to talk about it.

We were planning a visit. It had been a while. It was a relatively relaxed period in Djeli's schedule, for once, and he wanted to spend a little time in Bamako hanging out with me and visiting with the kids. Mariam had been surprisingly mellow recently. We were hoping we could have an uneventful week at this nice hotel called Le Djenné. Djeli had booked us adjoining rooms. We thought he could spend the afternoons with Issa and Farka at Mariam's house while I got some writing done, and then we'd have the evenings to spend together.

When I booked my flight, I decided that instead of hanging out at CDG for a long layover, I'd spend one night at a hotel in Paris. It would break up the trip and I'd arrive in Bamako less fried. On the RER into the city, I checked my BlackBerry. You already know what was on it. Nothing from Djeli. I dropped my stuff off at the hotel, met my old friend Susannah for dinner, texted Sandro before I went to sleep, and woke up feeling relatively refreshed for my flight to Bamako.

When I checked in at Le Djenné, the receptionist told me that M. Kouyaté hadn't yet checked into his room but that it was the one next door to mine. That was okay – I wanted to freshen up anyway. I didn't text him right away. I figured he was with the kids and I wanted to respect his time with them. I took a long lukewarm shower and rubbed some lotion into my skin. I was hungry but I figured I'd wait for Djeli so we could get some dinner together. I got dressed.

By 8:30 I was getting really famished. I'd been distractedly reading *Petals of Blood* but I kept stopping to check the BlackBerry. I was starting to get a little pissed off. I told the receptionist to tell Djeli when he got in that I'd gone out to get something to eat. Things were just starting to warm up in the neighborhood. Nightlife in Bamako gets going on the late side. I wandered over to the Bar Bla Bla, which looked like one of the livelier spots in the *quartier*. There was a motley assortment of Rastas and Peace Corps types. I figured I wouldn't stand out, particularly. I took a table in the corner and ordered the capitaine brochettes with a Coke.

There was a couple making out near the bathroom. He had her pressed up against the wall and their kisses looked very sweet. She was fat and pretty, and he was very skinny. She smiled a lot between their kisses. Djeli and I never kiss in public.

My fish was very good.

When I got back to the hotel, Djeli still hadn't appeared. I tried to read some more, and when that didn't work, I tried pretending to be trying to sleep. Then I got up, stripped down to my black lace panties, and posed in several provocative positions for myself in the full-length mirror. I looked pretty good.

Then I tried to read some more.

I finally gave in at 1 a.m. and texted Djeli the following message: "*donne-moi un signe de vie.*" I checked the BlackBerry fairly obsessively for the next hour, then cried for about five minutes, brushed my teeth, washed off my make-up, put on some moisturizer, turned out the light, and got in bed. I have some vague recollection of irritably swatting at a mosquito buzzing around my ear shortly before I drifted off.

Djeli, meanwhile, was snoozing in a first class seat on an airplane flying toward Charles de Gaulle International Airport. Issa and Farka were by his side, out cold. Mariam had thought he was overreacting, but as he had written me (though I hadn't read it), he just thought it would be better to have them in Paris until the outbreak was under control. And as he'd also written me, even if he couldn't be stroking my pussy on his bed at Le Djenné as we'd planned, he'd be in Paris before I knew it. He'd already asked Ama to make up the guestroom for me.

* * *

Monday, October 22, 2007, 10:47 p.m.
Subject: how to change the subject

Well, that's a funny way to make the "conversation seem finished: it's about the clitoris and the vagina." It finishes like this? I have to wait until November 1st to respond in person?

I went to see a brilliant play by an Israeli playwright, Hanoch Levin. "Krum." A Polish theater company, TR Warszawa. It gave you the impression that Polish people are extremely sexy, smart and ironic.

I'm just changing the topic to the theater in order to stop thinking about my clitoris and vagina.

This was so typical of Tzipi. I guess I started it. I'd sent her three little webcam photos of me masturbating while reading an e-mail she'd sent. They didn't show my head. Whenever I send dirty pictures to the paramour, I always leave them headless. It just seems like a good idea, considering how digital information travels. So these pictures were low-resolution, at an awkward angle, entirely home-made — and for this reason very sexy, if I say so myself. Tzipi didn't say anything about them. She just sent some kind of political tirade, which is sometimes what she does when she's aroused. I knew that's what was going on. So I wrote her, "I'm not even going to ask you what you thought of my pictures. I'm going to take that politically incorrect subject heading of yours as an indication of your arousal, because that's the way you are." She wrote back saying that my pictures made her very aroused. And that she wanted to talk with me about masturbation.

All of this was just a week and a half before we'd be seeing each other again. I asked her if she wanted to have this conversation when we saw each other, or if she wanted to have it on the internet, which was, as far as I could tell, created precisely for this kind of thing. We started having the conversation in our correspondence. I reminded her of an e-mail I'd once sent her about coming with my two fingers inside myself, imagining what she'd be feeling if my fingers were her fingers. She wrote back that she remembered that e-mail very well, and she loved it, and she had a question for me, but that she'd really rather talk about it than write about it. But she said, "Just to make the conversation seem finished: it's about the clitoris and the vagina."

And I kind of sort of changed the subject to the Polish theater company. Of course the conversation wasn't finished at all.

Tzipi wrote again, telling me a beautiful story about standing and looking at herself in the mirror when she was a little girl, and being aroused by her own tiny breasts and long hair, and imagining a little penis rising between her legs. This image reminded me of those magical drawings by Henry Darger, of little warrior girls with penises. I sent her a couple of photographs of these drawings. She seemed to like them. And then she made those interesting comments about reflexivity, and reflexive verbs in Romance languages, and masturbation. Of course, it wasn't "fellation" she shrugged off, but the "estimulation" of the G-spot, an anatomical invention she found highly suspect. I thought maybe this was a generational difference. I can tell you, with her two fingers inside of me, I know she's touched mine. She's willing to acknowledge that breasts are sensitive, that lips are sensitive, that all kinds of touch can be sensual, but she insists that female orgasm is almost inevitably linked to clitoral stimulation. Sometimes she'll go after mine – or her own – with a concentration bordering on hostility. Sometimes I'll grab her fingers and look into her eyes, and guide her to touch me with more delicacy. But the truth is, my erotic bond with Tzipi is so strong, even though we seem to disagree about some things in bed, I always come with her, immediately and repeatedly, and I always want more. Every time I'm near her I want to be touching her.

She says her fingers inside me are for her, not for me. She says she's imagining her cock deep inside of me. Sometimes when I send her dirty pictures, or messages about sex, she'll tell me I've given her a hard-on. Tzipi often refers to her own sexual excitation in masculine terms. Actually, sometimes I do that myself. In fact, I just got my own hard-on thinking about Tzipi's.

I'm not sure what she talks about with her analyst. I imagine they've discussed the mirror stage. It makes perfect sense, of course, that she sees a Lacanian. And yet I can't help but wonder sometimes if this is the best approach, from a therapeutic perspective. Because one of the things that seems to preoccupy her most is the sad truth of that infinite chain of signifiers – the infinite replaceability of her lovers. She's fundamentally a very committed person. Her love for Asher is profound. She still loves Hannah, in spite of everything. Pitzi too, of course. She's a dedicated friend to her circle of progressive and sensitive intellectuals. She's taken risks to defend them. But she's a very seductive person, and even though she complains on occasion about the bother or even terror of men and women falling in love with her, she can't really resist seducing them.

Especially young people. Now there's a little something for the analyst to chew on.

In this respect, Tzipi bears an uncanny resemblance to Simone de Beauvoir. There are a lot of stories about both her and Sartre. Of course she kind of told one of them herself in *She Came to Stay*. You know, the young woman they seduced and shared and then belittled wrote a pretty bitter response herself. There are also some rumors about the adopted daughter who published the letters. This is one reason I wonder about her assertion that she was "carrying out her mother's will" when she published her letters to Algren with all the embarrassing orthographic and grammatical errors she'd expressly said she wanted excised. Anyway, I can't say I'm sorry the letters were published this way.

In January of 1948, Simone de Beauvoir wrote to Algren a description of a New Year's party she'd been to. There was a charming fifteen-year-old girl there, and Simone describes the way she danced. She says that she imagines that if she were a man, she'd be a "very wicked" one because she'd surely take great pleasure in seducing and making love to young girls, and then she'd dump them immediately because they'd begin to get on her nerves. She says, "I feel there is both something appealing and something nauseating in very young girls."

This is precisely Tzipi's feeling about that "beautiful, dumb Thai girl." Of course, Simone de Beauvoir didn't need to be a "very wicked man" to seduce and dump a lot of beautiful young people. She managed just fine as a woman.

Do I sound bitter myself? I don't feel bitter – and I certainly can't claim to be an ingénue. When I met Tzipi I'd been around the block. Although she's twenty-three years older than me, I'm at the antique end of her spectrum. And I'm not dumb. Even Tzipi's acknowledged that. I went into this with my eyes wide open, and she's been honest with me every step of the way.

I told you, I have no idea why I got a little reckless with my emotions with her, when I'd managed to be so self-contained with the paramour.

I've been listening to that beautiful Bill Evans album, *Conversations with Myself*. Maybe you can see why this album interests me. It was considered very innovative when he recorded it in 1963, but also a little gimmicky. Evans laid down one solo piano track, and then laid down another on top of that, and then a third. Technically, it's very virtuosic. I mean his piano technique – the recording technique was really just piping these three tracks through a left, a right, and a middle channel. It sounds best if you have your speakers arranged far apart so you get that illusion of spatiality.

The most lyrical song on the album is the "Love Theme from *Spartacus*." In fact, if I were to choose a song to represent my love affair with Tzipi, it would be this song. I know that sounds pretty tacky. The theme song from a cheesy old movie with Kirk Douglas played on a gimmicky three-track album. But if you listen to it, you'll see what I mean. And *Spartacus*, of course, isn't just cheesy. It's actually kind of great. I watched it recently and at several moments I got tears in my eyes. It's not the love story, of course, that's moving. That part is pretty banal. It's the politics of it. It's so interesting that the first slave who sacrifices himself in order to make a statement about the brutality of slavery is a black man. That self-sacrifice is what politicizes Kirk Douglas, and turns him into a great revolutionary figure. There's the whole gay subplot with Tony Curtis (Laurence Olivier's "body slave"). And then there's the amazing scene when the soldiers come to the camp of rebel slaves and say they'll kill everyone unless Spartacus gives himself up. Kirk Douglas, of course, steps forward, chin first: "I am Spartacus." And then one by one, each of his comrades in arms also steps forth, willing to sacrifice himself for the higher cause. "I am Spartacus." "I am Spartacus." "I am Spartacus."

But the song, "Love Theme from *Spartacus*," the way that Bill Evans plays it, isn't dramatic this way. What's beautiful about it, the reason I find it so *à propos* of my relationship with Tzipi, is that it begins so lush and sentimental, so tender, ultra-sensitive – and then it changes character entirely and becomes funny, be-bop, clever, sexy, playful. I get sentimental over Tzipi, but she's so smart that however cruel or hard-headed or selfish she can be, in the end I always find myself smiling at her virtuosity.

She wrote me about a month ago about a twenty-one-year-old couple she'd met at a reading she gave at Tel Aviv University with Tanya Reinhart. Afterwards she took the young couple home with her and the three of them had sex – she and the boy took turns working on his girlfriend. She said they were both beautiful and intelligent, and that this encounter was "very important." But she hasn't said anything about them since then.

In the "Seminar" on Poe, Lacan asks this interesting question: "For a purloined letter to exist, we may ask, to whom does a letter belong?" He notes that there are certain situations in which the sender might reasonably feel some proprietary rights regarding the letter which he's written, even if he sends it to the recipient, ostensibly, as a gift. Clearly, there are both legal and ethical ramifications to this observation which spring to mind. But Lacan is more interested in the psychological ramifications. This is related to that complicated assertion that "a letter always arrives at its destination," even if the recipient never gets it. Because, as Lacan suggests, it may well be that the person to whom the letter was addressed was never "the real receiver."

I thought a lot about this while I was reading Simone de Beauvoir's correspondence with Nelson Algren, and *not* reading Nelson Algren's correspondence with Simone de Beauvoir.

Monday, October 29, 2007, 9:59 a.m.
Subject: Darger

Good morning. Today I'm sending you the beautiful pictures by Henry Darger. Henry Darger was a crazy person who lived alone and secretly wrote a book that was 15,000 pages long. They found it when he was dying. He made thousands of pictures to illustrate the story. He would copy drawings of little girls out of magazine advertisements, and he gave them all penises and testicles. Half the time they were naked.

The story is full of action and kind of frightening. The girls have to fight a lot of battles. You can see, some of the drawings are very violent. Anyway, I thought of these girls when you wrote about looking at yourself in the mirror, and the penis you imagined popping out.

And that made me remember Freud's essay, "A Child Is Being Beaten," which is about a very typical fantasy construct of girls. First the girl fantasizes that another child, often her brother or sister, is being beaten by the father. Freud says this is a way for her to fantasize that she is loved exclusively, or best, by the father. Then the fantasy becomes masochistic: she is the one being beaten herself. The fantasy is often accompanied by masturbation. The girl usually forgets this middle phase of the fantasy (it is shameful), and ends with a more abstract but sexually exciting sense that "a child is being beaten" - not her, nor a brother or sister, just "a child."

Feminist psychoanalytic theorists like this essay because they say it's one of the places where Freud suggests that one's gender identification can slip and change. The masturbatory fantasy of the girl is linked to her shifting identification with the child-figures who move from boy to girl and back again.

Speaking of Freud, and penises, I learned a new dirty expression: "smoking a Cuban." It means giving a blow-job with the active use of both hands. Of course when I heard that it made me think of you, and that photograph on your desk of you and Harry Mathews smoking Cubans in the marché des enfants rouges.

Last night I went with Florence to see Karen Finley perform. Do you know who she is? She became very famous because in the 1990s conservative politicians here protested the fact that she received government funds to produce work they found "obscene" (there were 3 other artists implicated but she was the most talked-about because of something involving yams). It went all the way to the Supreme Court and they ended up taking away the funding. And then she was very famous for being obscene.

She is obscene. She is also fantastic and beautiful and sexual, and hysterical in the fullest sense of the term, and frightening and funny and deeply sad. I was very moved.

It's getting colder, but it's nice: crisp, with a very blue sky. I think it will be like this when you get to Boston.

xoxo

Tzipi was going to give a talk at Harvard and she invited me up to stay at the hotel with her for two nights. As usual, she'd booked us adjoining rooms. As I said, she liked those pictures by Darger that I sent her. But she wasn't particularly interested in the business about Freud. Even though she's in analysis, it really bothers her when I start in with my Freudian mallet. And she has no patience at all for French feminist theory about the slippery slope of gender identity. *Of course* Tzipi considers herself a feminist, but it's hard to say what that means, exactly. Her politics are very unpredictable.

In one of her letters to Algren, Simone de Beauvoir makes some reference to the fact that he didn't identify as a Jew, or that he acknowledged being Jewish but in a strange way, and the editor explained that in an interview he had said jokingly that he was a "Swedish Jew," which was his way of saying that technically he was both of these things but that he didn't really identify as either. This was funny, because when Tzipi was very young, that actress Tippi Hedren was very popular, and Tzipi used to joke that she was going to change her name to Tzipi Hedren, because she thought she was really Swedish. Because of her very public position on Palestine, a lot of people have accused Tzipi of being a "self-hating Jew." She's not, of course. She's just a Swedish Jew. I'm not sure what kind of feminist she is.

We were planning a visit. Tzipi was spending a few weeks on Mykonos, working on the manuscript of *Problems are Defiant like Unattractive Angels*. She'd rented a little villa that had a guestroom. She invited me to spend a few days with her. The messages Tzipi sent me from Greece were glorious. Of course we talked more about Sappho, and about Nietzsche. She shares my enthusiasm for *The Birth of Tragedy*. I told her that from a distance, before I met her, she'd always struck me as a Bacchante, but when I got to know her I realized how Apollinian she was. She said, "Oh, I am very Apollinian." I told her about a film documentation I'd seen of Richard Schechner's famous theatrical production, *Dionysus in '69*. The actual production was done in 1968. It was based on *The Bacchae*, but the hippie actors would suddenly slip out of character and say their real names and talk like cool cats, and make references to sex, drugs, and rock 'n' roll. They acted out a Native American birthing ritual in the nude, and then they started playing bongo drums and making out with the audience. The film was shot by Brian de Palma before he became famous. I guess then he was just a guy with a camera – or actually, two cameras. It was a split screen. The whole thing was very hallucinogenic and sexy and could never happen today. I'm kind of jealous that Tzipi got to be a part of that generation.

I sent her an image from *Dionysus in '69* which I found very beautiful. It's the birthing ceremony:

I said I knew it was funny for me to be sending this image enthusiastically, because I'd earlier had that exchange with her about how I found the idea of group sex overly distracting. That exchange about "focus." I, who seemed so Apollinian, was showing my Dionysian side. And she, who really looked the part of the Bacchante, had come out as Apollinian.

Tzipi quoted to me a passage from *The Birth of Tragedy* about a counterintuitive optical phenomenon: "When after a forceful attempt to gaze on the sun we turn away blinded, we see dark-colored spots before our eyes, as a cure, as it were. Conversely, the bright image projections of the Sophoclean hero – in short, the Apollinian aspect of the mask – are necessary effects of a glance into the inside and terrors of nature; as it were, luminous spots to cure eyes damaged by gruesome night."

She wrote me some other beautiful things – about the ocean, about the smell of salt and the shock of the white villas against the intense turquoise sky, about the lemony taste of the fish and the calm of the nights there, about how she wanted to touch my thighs and my belly and feel my small, hard nipple between her lips. She also told me there was a local girl named Melina who'd developed an obsession with her. Tzipi told me it was entertaining at first because she was pretty and had big brown eyes and a nice ass and she liked to dance around the terrace for Tzipi but it was a little hard to get her to leave after fucking and she'd told her I was coming and pretty soon she was going to have to clear out and she'd cried. Tzipi told me she was telling me this because she wanted to tell me everything as it was a way of being close to me. That was the one message from Greece that didn't make me feel particularly close to her, but as I said, she's been honest with me every step of the way.

When I flew in to Athens, I had about a four hour layover. I checked my BlackBerry. We don't need to go over what was on there. On Mykonos, I got a taxi out to the villa. She wasn't there but the door was open. The place was kind of a mess. That surprised me a little but I figured she'd been concentrating on writing the novel. I found the guestroom and began to make myself at home. I took a shower. I put on those thigh-high stockings, my black lace panties, and a little black shift. I put on make-up. I lay on the bed and waited. I checked the BlackBerry. Nothing. I texted Sandro and told him to study hard for his algebra exam. It got dark and I drifted off for a little bit. When I heard the door to the patio open, I was sure it was Tzipi, but it wasn't.

Tzipi was just arriving in Athens, having written me that Melina was having a very inconvenient reaction to being dumped. She told me not to bother to catch the connecting flight, that she'd already booked us adjoining rooms at the King George in Athens, and it was too bad I'd missed the villa but she couldn't wait to show me the Acropolis anyway. And she said that even if she couldn't be stroking my pussy on Mykonos as we'd planned, we'd be together tonight in Athens and it gave her a very hard wood just thinking about it.

CHAPTER 3: ANIMAL CRACKERS

I think I'd like to explain that earlier comment I made about bonobos. If you'll recall, a couple of years ago I sent an e-mail to Binh with an *obscene* picture of a female bonobo masturbating. I got the picture off the internet. Here it is:

I sent it because we'd recently had a humorous exchange about bonobos and sex. It was during one of our discussions of sexual jealousy. He'd shared with me some anecdote about a recent adventure he'd had, and he expressed interest in hearing about my own activities. He said hearing about that kind of thing turned him on. By now you've observed that my sex life is, as it were, a half-open book, but I wasn't quite so sure that all this sharing of details between us was a good idea. I said that I thought that sexual possessiveness was politically objectionable and a bad idea in practical terms, but that didn't mean I didn't experience a twinge of it sometimes. I wondered if his own desire to hear about my sex with other people wasn't just a little masochistic.

He answered by saying his attitude toward the subject was very much like that of bonobos. He explained that bonobo males frequently deal with sexual jealousy by sending away the female under dispute, and then seeking out the male rival. Then the two males have sex together. It seems this resolves the tension. He said that the females sometimes did something along these lines, but with less frequency. Evidently, the females just generally rub their vulvas up against other females' vulvas in an ordinary, friendly way, so they don't need triangulation as an excuse. (He also described the male-on-male maneuvers most typically performed: back-to-back, they rub their scrotal sacks together.) Binh said that bonobos were famous for resolving all kinds of social conflict through sex, as opposed to violence.

I found this compelling. I did a little internet research, and everything seemed to confirm what Binh had said. This being an historic moment of clearly regrettable decisions regarding political violence as a means to "resolve" social conflict, it was hard not to agree that the bonobos seemed to have found a better way. I also, as I wrote Binh, did an image search on Google, which is where I discovered this astonishing picture of the female masturbating. As you would expect, I experienced a profound sense of identification when I saw her.

There were only two problems with this whole exchange. The first was that, in spite of the heartening story of the bonobos' political life, I still found Binh's anecdotes regarding his sexual adventures to be a little bit painful. The second was that he didn't leave well enough alone with the compelling story above. He wanted to push the human-animal sexual comparison a little further, and pretty soon he was citing Darwin in order to suggest that it was "natural" that I would experience somewhat more discomfort around sexual jealousy than he because (I'm sure you've heard this argument before) in evolutionary terms, women stood a better chance of reproducing through monogamous, consistent sexual relations than men, whose chances increase if they spread around their seed.

While I was happy to identify with the female bonobo in that photograph, I was entirely disinclined to buy into the all-too-familiar Darwin story. While I've already told you that Binh is a genius, there are times he says things that make him look really dumb. Or maybe just really young.

In October of 1948, Simone de Beauvoir wrote to Nelson Algren, "Honey, did you really fall on the head at eight months old? It would explain many things."

Despite some evidence of immaturity, I have to admit, Binh is a very good father. You should see him hopping around like a frog with Bao and Bob. When he's with the kids, all his more trivial preoccupations seem to evaporate. He handles their little bodies with such confident tenderness. They climb on him and nuzzle into his neck. He cooks them mashed organic yams, reads them stories, tickles them just enough, brushes their tiny teeth, and puts them to sleep by lying down with them and softly stroking their coppery hair and measuring his breathing against theirs. He loves them so much.

He's always a little sad when it's time to send them back to their mother's house. But then he gets back to his more mundane preoccupations: having his photo taken for the Gap ad campaign; deciding whether to sign that public letter on Darfur; rescheduling a "play date" with those two young art students he met when he gave a crit at the UdK; editing the new music video for Ponytail; figuring out whether to go to Dieter's party for Lenny Kravitz (Aafke might show up).

And of course, there's his art. You must be wondering about that night at Propeller Island. You'll recall that we left Binh sleeping peacefully in his padded cell, while I, like our female bonobo friend in the photograph, attempted to take care of myself. But while she appears to be utterly unselfconscious, tranquil, and self-possessed, my own activities in the lion cage were anxious, theatrical, thrashing, and pitiful.

There was more to the spam-trapped e-mail. For once, Binh had decided to incorporate our romance into a conceptual art project. And yet I was still not to appear. He explained that he'd had a huge screen erected in Potsdamer Platz, with a high-power digital projector located across the plaza. He'd carefully positioned four surveillance cameras inside the lion cage at different strategic angles. These were hooked up for a live-feed to the Potsdamer Platz projector. The project, part of his new "Nocturnal Emissions" series, was to begin at midnight. Alternating in one-minute intervals between the perspectives of the four surveillance cameras, the live-feed would project various lonely images of the empty cage where we had planned to meet, but didn't, with a scrolling text at the bottom of the screen saying, "Picture me having sex with my lover in the room next door."

Of course, everything went as planned for the first hour and fifteen minutes. Binh had dropped off to sleep waiting for me. He's not the type to get particularly worked up about a friend's tardy arrival, and there's something very soporific, I'm sure you can imagine, about lying around in a padded cell. It obviously wasn't going to make a big difference for the projection if we actually were or weren't having sex in the room for crazy people.

When I entered the cage and began my little call-of-the-wild routine, it took a few minutes for anybody to even notice what was going on. The intern manning the projector positioned in a fifteenth floor office across the plaza was drinking a can of pilsner and playing Tetris on his cell phone. Then there was a bit of confusion when he got a call from security, and wondered if he should call and wake the curator to ask if Binh had mentioned a change of plans. When he did call, the curator hesitated for a moment, and then decided, reasonably, that it would be easier to claim technical difficulties and shut the thing down than to risk obscenity charges.

I was only really up on that massive screen for a total of about six minutes. The video and stills captured on the digital devices of curious passersby were fortunately censored before they could make it to YouTube, and besides, the surveillance camera images were highly pixelated. I wouldn't have been recognizable to anybody except maybe Sandro and Florence, who knew about my costuming plans. The whole thing blew over fairly quickly, and Binh wasn't even particularly disturbed to lose sponsorship for the "Nocturnal Emissions" series which, he ultimately decided (and rightly, I have to say) was a trite idea.

"Auf anderthalb Meter hohen Stelzen stehen die beiden Käfige im Zentrum der großzügigen Manege und warten auf den Applaus vom Nachbargast. Ihr Vorhang entscheidet, was das Publikum sieht!"

It's funny that while Binh claims to be "Swedish-Vietnamese," I am, in fact, the one with a Swedish grandmother. As I'm sure you know, there's a large Scandinavian population in the Midwest. I don't have those extreme Nordic looks that Aafke does. My eyes aren't pale blue like hers, but a kind of indeterminate greenish-grey. My skin is actually a little tawny, and my hair is brown. In fact, of all of my grandparents, my Swedish grandmother was the darkest one. She was olive-skinned, with black eyes and black hair. My mother vaguely explained this at some point in my childhood. She said something about how the Vikings had gone raping and pillaging a lot of "island maidens," leaving some of us Swedes with these traces of those other exotic realms.

In the course of my relationship with Binh, Sandro, of course, has been growing up. Maybe you've registered some qualms that I communicate as openly as I do with him about certain aspects of my personal life. But Sandro also has that "old soul" thing going on. In fact, sometimes I think he's a little more mature than Binh. He's also pretty sexually precocious. He lost his virginity a few months ago.

Of course, the whole concept of "virginity" I find entirely suspect. I wrote about this to Binh. It followed a brief, flirtatious exchange we'd had about a couple of sexual possibilities we hadn't yet actualized with each other. And never would. Perhaps it will surprise you to learn, after reading that Binh wrote so enthusiastically about the creative bonobo maneuvers, that there are other acts, besides fellatio, that leave him cold.

Monday, November 5, 2007, 2:43 p.m.
Subject: eye contact

And speaking of squeamish, you crack me up with your cups of tea. I think it's also hilarious that you claim to be so much more homosexual than me. Je crois que je suis bien plus pédée que tu es lesbien.

102

I had a beautiful conversation with Sandro about sex. I said that I thought it was great that he'd had sex with his girlfriend, but that in fact, it was very arbitrary to think that the penis-vagina sex act was "real" sex. They'd already done everything you can do with the combination mouth – fingers – vagina – penis, except for that. Now there's that. I said that the truth was that these other things could be even more intimate. He said, "Yeah, it's true, and who said that sex had to be through touch? What about eye contact? Or talking?" But he's very happy to have put his penis in her vagina.

I was teasing you when I called you Anaïs Nin. Besides, I like Anaïs Nin.

You may be getting increasingly uncomfortable about the juxtaposition of writing about sex with my lover with writing about my son. Indeed, this may well be worrisome. Perhaps it's even more worrisome that the photograph I showed you of "Binh's nipple" – the one that looked like an eye – in fact belonged to Sandro. The other morning when he was dressing for school I said, "Before you put on your shirt, can I take a picture of your nipple? It's for the novel I'm writing. Binh is supposed to send me a picture of his nipple in an e-mail."

In addition to the fact that this little role-play game is of questionable taste, it is really ballsy of me to pretend to be a digital art star, with my little pink Sony Cyber-shot, an antiquated webcam, and some cheapo digital image enhancement software that came with tacky templates for greeting cards and calendars. Florence, who is a painter, has pointed out to me that the "hot young art star" is probably the most clichéd and overdone character in this novel.

The truth is, the paramour has never sent me a digital image in an e-mail – much less a .mov file. I, on the other hand, have sent any number of pictures. As I said, I decapitate the dirty ones. I have sent my own nipple. But I send pictures of a lot of other things. Bonobos. Some of my vaguely perverse knitting and crochet projects. Sexual looking flowers.

Actually, it began with flowers. It was toward the beginning of our correspondence, and I was still trying to suss out to what degree the paramour was interested in something romantic, or at least sexual, with me. In a gesture of friendliness, I'd offered to send an iPod holder I'd crocheted. I said, "If you don't want to carry an iPod in it, you can use it to hold a pack of cigarettes (but don't smoke)." We were still exchanging information about some of our habits, our basic likes and dislikes, our intellectual and aesthetic stances, and desires. I couldn't ask outright, of course, about sex. So I sent this e-mail:

Sunday, July 31, 2005, 5:16 p.m.
Subject: pure or impure

It's only fair that you should make some mistakes in English, since I make mistakes all the time in French.

I think it's funny and nice you don't have an iPod. I'm very happy you don't smoke. I didn't think so. If you have to have one of these habits, I recommend the iPod.

You and Sandro like Beethoven. I prefer Bach. Monk and Evans and the rest, this was also my formation. After I discovered Steve Reich in college, I became interested in West African music. I vaguely know some of the rockers you mentioned.

It's beautiful here. Yesterday I spent the day shopping at the farmers' market and gardening on the terrace. I wanted to send you a picture of a flower. I couldn't decide: pure or impure? So I'm sending both. One I grew and one I bought.

I hope you're not offended by dirty pictures.

I appended a shot of the perky little smiley-faced pansies from my balcony, and the scandalously sexual iris I'd bought. The paramour played dumb, merely responding that there was nothing "dirty" about these photos – they were merely "sensual," as flowers often were, "principally orchids."

It wasn't until we'd actually slept together a couple of months later that I started considering sending impure pictures of myself. Actually, they were very pure. Even the one of my labia. That labial flower from the farmers' market was much more obscene.

I apologize for the thoroughly counterfeit and not even particularly convincing facsimile of Binh's non-existent artistic interventions into our correspondence. It's hard to know how to do this tastefully.

Simone de Beauvoir also struggled with how to write about, or not write about, Algren. She went on to depict their love affair in a novel, *The Mandarins*. According to what she wrote Algren about that process, she left out a few details but on the whole stayed pretty close to the truth. Then years later, in a nonfiction work called *Force of Circumstance*, she was quite explicit about some of the more sensitive things that had happened between them. That's when Algren pretty much lost it. He made some very angry statements to the press, which he evidently regretted later. Even very early on in their correspondence, Simone was already worrying about how to depict him – how much she could say, and how much she couldn't say. She was writing a book about her travels through the US, and she didn't know how to deal with narrating the events when she got to Chicago. She felt it would be somehow inappropriate to write about the initiation of their love affair, but it was difficult to talk about her experience of Chicago without somehow referencing Algren.

She wrote him, "Well, I have to find a way of saying the truth without saying it; that is exactly what is literature, after all: clever lies which secretly say the truth."

So I hope you will forgive me if I tell you that after that catastrophe with the giant-screen projection of my supreme humiliation, Binh evidenced first a somewhat childish indifference, but in the aftermath, when he came to understand what it had cost me, he showed a tenderness that was unlike anything he'd ever expressed before.

I had told him once that I knew that our sexual relationship was precarious, and that due to his constitutional disability and my own instinct for self-preservation, we clearly wouldn't be falling in love anytime soon. But I said, "Who knows, sometimes I think we could fall in love when you're sixty, and I'm eighty-three." That, I could imagine. So after he'd shrugged off the Potsdamer Platz fiasco, after I wept and fretted (unnecessarily, it turned out) about the potential personal and professional ramifications, after he finally held me sobbing in his arms and realized what I'd suffered, he wrote me a very beautiful message saying that who knew, when we were sixty and eighty-three, maybe indeed we'd be lovers, or ex-lovers, or dear friends, or collaborators, but we certainly couldn't be far from one another.

* * *

Of course it didn't happen like that. The paramour has never seen me cry. Well, there was that one time when Djeli played the kora in bed and his heartbreakingly sensitive response to his own song prompted a small, subtle, sympathetic tear to roll down my cheek. But in general, I do my best to hold it together with the paramour, even on e-mail. That short "I'm irritated with you" message was about as emotive as I ever got. But my lover did seem to feel for me for a minute there after the catastrophe.

You may be wondering if we've had any contact in recent days. In fact, not. I responded to that message about the shrink with something light and amiable, and nothing came back. As I said, not getting messages these days is something of a relief. I'm working on this manuscript fairly obsessively.

I did, however, take some time out today to go to see a play with Sandro. It was a company called Elevator Repair Service, and they were doing a very interesting adaptation of Faulkner's *The Sound and the Fury*. We've seen this company before, and they're always quirky and inventive. Sandro's taste runs toward the avant-garde. I once wrote the paramour that in general, I liked my art "small and experimental." My lover responded that "small and experimental" was good, but so was "big and experimental." I think this was meant to imply that a fan-base in the hundreds of thousands or even millions didn't mean that the paramour was not experimenting. In fact this is true. But I've already mentioned my lover's fascination with popular culture – that business about Cameron Diaz, for example. I myself don't find fame for the sake of fame quite so captivating.

Anyway, we very much enjoyed *The Sound and the Fury*. It focused on the section of the novel narrated by Benjy, the "idiot" Compson son, so of course it was disjunctive, non-linear, and sometimes confusing. In this production, each character was represented by a couple of different actors, often of contrasting race and gender. That opened up some interesting interpretive possibilities, and shifted around the political implications. There was also some highly stylized and comical choreography. The woman who played Benjy for most of the production was a wiry, child-like, bird-faced actress. I also saw her play Jack Kerouac (excellent).

Naturally, seeing this play made me want to come home and take another look at Faulkner. I'd also been thinking about

Faulkner because of Simone de Beauvoir's letters to Nelson Algren. You may be aware that Sartre wrote a very famous essay on Faulkner arguing that *The Sound and the Fury* manifested many of the tenets of existentialism. But in their correspondence, Simone de Beauvoir is constantly assuring Algren that he is a superior novelist to virtually all of his compatriots, including Faulkner. This makes you wonder if her opinion wasn't influenced by the fact that Algren was good in bed. She does, at one point, say that she and Sartre are going to publish a piece by Faulkner in *Les Temps modernes*. She says, "It is good since he has the Nobel Prize." As you know, Tzipi Honigman also won the Nobel Prize. Simone de Beauvoir won the Prix Goncourt for *The Mandarins*. Relative to Faulkner, Nelson Algren was the kind of person Carlo would classify as a "loser."

"Clearly, for Faulkner, writing is a kind of doubling in which the author's self is reconstituted within the realm of language as the Other, a narcissistic mirroring of the self to which the author's reaction is at once a fascinated self-love and an equally fascinated self-hatred." – John T. Irwin, in the Norton Critical Edition of *The Sound and the Fury*

Thursday, December 6, 2007, 11:28 p.m.
Subject: your pick

Choose one:

a) After my show in Tokyo last week, all I wanted to do was see my kids and I can't think about anything else right now. I'll ask Kadidia to send that cream. My shoe size is 43.

b) My dear friend, I'm really sorry you suffered so much in

Bamako all alone. I'd like to write a longer message but I've been very busy and I'm exhausted. Everything will be all right, I promise, I've already talked with my sister, and with Dr. Touré. They said this is the typical healing process and nothing to be concerned about. The cream will come. I'm not sleeping well, but I read the beautiful little book about masturbation and I thought of you with desire. My children are beautiful and are making me happy. I hope you and Sandro are well, aside from the obvious. Fabienne is doing much better. I will be very glad to see you here in January. My feet are medium in size. Bisous.

c) I've had it, enough with hallucinating, needy, scabby chicks, I am indeed a dreadlocked SpongeBob, I spend half my time in a tropical country, I don't need wool socks.

I sent this in the aftermath of the fiasco. While it's true that immediately afterwards Djeli had shown uncharacteristic warmth and solicitude, within a couple of weeks he'd slipped back into his customary role of unreliable, sporadic correspondent. I was really worried about how my sores were going to heal once all the scabs had fallen off. My doctor here in New York was vaguely reassuring but since he didn't have a lot of experience with tropical diseases, I wasn't sure he was the best source. Djeli had mentioned that his sister Kadidia had suggested a very effective herbal cream and she'd be happy to send some. He'd also spoken with his own GP in Bamako, Dr. Touré, and he also thought this cream would be helpful. Djeli, naturally, never followed up on it. I asked him if he could. I also asked him if he'd heard anything about Fabienne's health.

In my recuperation period, I read a lovely little book by Harry Mathews about masturbation and I asked Sandro to mail it to Djeli when I was done. I also knit a lot of socks. I began making a beautiful pair for Djeli with a pale green wool fingerling yarn, but handmade socks really need to be made to measure. I asked Djeli for his shoe size.

A letter to the editor had recently come out in a music magazine that took issue with one of the wacko political statements that Djeli occasionally makes. The author of the letter had perhaps not fully understood the implicit irony in Djeli's comment, or maybe he'd actually understood it perfectly and still found it idiotic. In any event, he called Djeli a "dreadlocked SpongeBob SquarePants." Djeli seemed to like this.

So, as the days passed, there was no word on the cream, no thanks for the book, no reassuring news regarding Fabienne, and, to add insult to injury, no indication of the size of Djeli's foot. I was stuck wondering whether to bind off the toe, or add another half inch. When I couldn't wait any longer, I sent him the three choices. He wrote back saying that all three were good. He talked about some other news but didn't actually answer any of my questions himself. I went with a European size 43. I assumed Fabienne was okay, since I was. Djeli never sent the cream. My sores healed just fine. I was left without a scar.

Sometimes when Djeli takes a while to write me, or writes something vaguely questionable, I write him, "Hm." He once asked about this. He wanted to make sure he was understanding it correctly. He said that in French, one sometimes said, "*Hmm*," as an alternative to, "*Bah, oueh…*" but that it wasn't generally written out in prose. He said when he read it in my messages, he imagined me smiling slightly and looking a little distrustful. I said, yes, that that was the appropriate reading. I said my "hm"s also implied a raising of one eyebrow. We had a similar exchange about the word *ahem*.

On account of his increasing reticence, I wrote him last month:

Wednesday, April 16, 2008, 9:16 a.m.
Subject: Ahem

In our relaxed and somewhat foul-mouthed household, when Sandro doesn't text me back, I write him, "DUDE YOU SUCK." Between me and Florence, all we have to do is send a Black-Berry e-mail that says "?!" and that usually prompts a quick 3-word assurance from the quiet person. With you, my strategy has been to compose optional replies for you to choose from, a, b, or c. But given that I had an inappropriate temper tantrum within my last menstrual cycle, I'm resigning myself to just prodding you periodically with polite but slightly wry one- or two-syllable onomatopoeic insertions in the chatty missives I send you when I feel like telling you something.

Djeli answered right away, a charming, warm, and informative message. Then he disappeared again.

You will have noticed the reference to a temper tantrum. Actually, that was the "I'm irritated with you" message. It's true that hormonal fluctuations may have some small impact on the tone of my correspondence. But for the first three years of my relationship with the paramour, I managed to keep this relatively under control. In fact, I don't think my crankiness had that much to do with my menstrual cycle. I think maybe I was just getting kind of tired of this.

I realize that you may be thinking, "It took her three years to wake up and smell the coffee?" I know that from what I've reproduced here, it might appear that my diligent commitment to the correspondence was all that was keeping it alive. But I'm not showing you what Djeli wrote me. I can only tell you that when he was good, as the saying goes, he was very very good. In fact, sometimes, in his lyrical, sideways style, he'd be so loving, I wasn't sure how to respond.

It's funny, I'm curious about what Nelson Algren wrote to Simone de Beauvoir, but I'm kind of glad I can't read it.

There was a pain and it was like a needle in the back of my eye and there were sharp colors and there was a smell. There was a knock and then a thud and the pain behind my eye and there was a woman standing over me and she was speaking French but I was understanding.

"Did you fall? I came to clean the room. *Est-ce que vous êtes malade?*"

There was a smell and the pain and I felt cold and hot all at once and then there were two other women and one of them was whispering, "*C'est la dengue, c'est la dengue.*"

My bones hurt and my eye hurt and the light was hot and sharp and the floor was hard and someone said, "*Comme elle gémit, c'est la dengue.*"

Somebody was lifting me and lifting me and my panties were wet and cold and I was cold but I was hot and someone wrapped a sheet around me and it smelled like bleach. And then she brushed my hair from my eyes and said, "It's okay, we're taking you to the clinic, it's just a fever, it's okay."

And they carried me and then there was the smell of gasoline and rubber and everything was shaking and my head felt like it was going to explode and I felt all my bones, it was like my bones were full of fire, and I was hot and I was cold and it smelled like rubbing alcohol.

And there was a bed and it was white and there was a curtain and it was white and it was blowing a little and the light was like a knife in my eyes and I closed them and a woman said, "*Comme elle gémit*, poor thing, *c'est la dengue.*"

There was a television near the ceiling and there were noises that hurt my head and there were shapes and colors but I couldn't see what they were supposed to be and the light was like a knife in my eyes and someone said, "Fabienne, you have a new roommate," and the girl named Fabienne moaned, and someone said, "*Comme elle pue.* Tell Fanta to clean her up."

It was night and the dark was moving like shapes, like animals, and I was afraid and I started to cry and Fabienne moaned and someone came and put some little pills in my mouth and made me swallow some water, and my skin felt like needles were going in it and I felt sick and I leaned over the bed and I was sick and Fanta came back to clean me up again and I slept.

In the morning the light was moving on the wall, it looked like leaves, and someone tried to feed me something but I had a hard time swallowing, I thought I was going to be sick again, and someone said, "*Comme elle bave,*" and it smelled like leaves.

And I peed in my bed and someone lifted me and someone cleaned me up and they put me back in a bed and it smelled like bleach and my head was heavy and I cried.

I'll spare you any more of my bad Faulkner impersonation. You get the idea. I had dengue fever – like everybody and his brother in Bamako that week. It was a raging epidemic, over almost as quickly as it began. My timing was impeccable: I'd gotten to town just as Djeli'd had the good sense to get the hell out. I spent five days in the hospital with my little roommate, Fabienne, a 12-year-old girl, coincidentally the daughter of a friend of Djeli's, with a case as bad as mine. The hotel maid had discovered me, passed out in the bathroom, the morning after my dinner at the Bar Bla Bla.

During my hospitalization, Sandro was blissfully ignorant. He told me afterwards that he didn't even miss getting my little harassment text messages about homework and piano. He figured I was just having too much fun with my Malian rock star. When

I didn't answer Florence's e-mail, she figured the same thing. Djeli, of course, was worried when I didn't turn up in Paris. He finally called the hotel and found out what had happened.

After three days of very trippy fever, diarrhea, and vomiting, I began to recognize my surroundings. Then came the rash. It started on my legs and wrists, then the red spots started coming out on my chest. They itched like crazy. There was pus coming out.

If you can avoid getting dengue fever, I'd recommend it.

Nothing like having scabs all over your body to make you feel de-eroticized. It was a while after that before I felt compelled to send another dirty picture to Djeli. But our correspondence isn't all about eroticism. As evidenced by the bits I've reproduced, a lot of it is about books and films, and politics. I think Djeli likes it that I sometimes challenge him on his wacky political positions. That is to say, many people have criticized him in the press about some of the seemingly contradictory things he's said, but in his day-to-day social life, he tends to surround himself with people who are willing to brush things aside on account of his lyricism and his personal charisma, or maybe (this is a more cynical assertion) his fame.

It's interesting that while people love to compare him to other national music icons, no one has ever called him "the Bob Marley of Mali." In point of fact, despite his hairstyle, Djeli has serious doubts about Rastafarianism. In his critique (in keeping with his critique of pretty much all organized religion), he never fails to raise the question of gender and sexual politics. That's all well and good, except that Djeli has a very cagey way of skirting the issue of his own relationship to these things. Cagey may not be the best word. Let's say, his argumentation is often circuitous. He's so smart, and his thinking is so subtle and complex, it's very hard to tell exactly what he's saying. He gave an interview on the topic of religion and sexuality which was, you might say, confusing. Somebody else responded that it looked like his politics were "spinning" from left to right. Djeli wrote me noting that if you actually examined the movement of the spheres, the world was spinning from right to left and he like the rest of us was going along for the ride. He was just trying to keep his bearings. I wrote him back:

Wednesday, December 7, 2005, 3:51 p.m.
Subject: the movement of the spheres

I'd already understood everything you said about that interview. The world doesn't spin from left to right and it's reductive to say you do – but let me think at least once in a while that some of your arguments leave a person a little dizzy, and it's not always helpful. The denial had a circular logic, and if you follow it, fine, maybe what you're saying is even more radical than the "politically correct" argument. But also, it's not. And if the world weren't also spinning the way it's going, maybe this wouldn't be a problem. But it is. When they "accused" Charlie Chaplin of being a Jew, he said, "Unfortunately, I don't have that honor." It was a simple response, maybe too simple, but it was beautiful. This story of yours is more complicated. Your way of thinking about it is very complicated.

I often have to laugh with Sandro, because his politics are hardly subtle. It's better to be black than to be white. It's better to be poor than rich, better to be gay than straight, better to be a woman than a man, better to be almost anything than American. But when I ask him if he'd really prefer to be a woman, he smiles and says that in truth, what he really loves is having a penis.

I think Djeli feels this way too.

Faulkner wrote that Benjy was "gelded" in 1913, after being inappropriately physically affectionate toward a passing schoolgirl, to whom he must have appeared monstrous. I realize that despite my moderation I may sometimes appear a little monstrous.

But maybe this sounds like me again with my Freud and my mallet. Honestly, I don't think I have penis envy. In the exchange that followed that e-mail, I told Djeli: "I love being a woman."

Both Sandro and Florence look at all this from a distance, and, maybe more than either Djeli or me, they actually do seem to manage to keep their bearings. That is to say, they both generously suspend judgment of either of us. I don't go into detail with them about the political arguments. They're aware, of course, of some of the controversies surrounding my lover, but they're both of the opinion that life is complex and we all say questionable things on occasion.

They also suspend judgment on some of the more questionable aspects of the ill-defined terms of my relationship with the paramour. When I do begin to squawk a little about how confusing this can be, they remind me that my lover has always been honest with me, every step of the way.

The rest of that e-mail about the movement of the spheres went like this:

It's funny, all this is about being too subtle, or not being subtle enough, and about disclosure and discretion. And I ended up thinking that on a personal level, as well, with me, you were either too subtle or not subtle enough, or that you said too much or not enough about your sex life. It's true that you talk a lot, and sometimes it's a little hard to follow your logic. (This doesn't bother me. The people I love the most are this way – my brother, Sandro – even me, when I start talking a lot, I sometimes find myself doing this.) I'm more of an exhibitionist than you, but you said more about sex. I'm not sure if it was too much or not enough.

Djeli wrote back that that was an elegant formulation, and he agreed.

* * *

Thursday, January 19, 2006, 1:08 p.m.
Subject: fossils

I had a long, beautiful conversation with an old friend of mine, E---- C----. He came over for tea. He told me about an essay he wrote with a Serbian woman about love and photography. And Barthes. I told him about my sonnets, and later we exchanged work. He told me he was in Israel last year, I think for the first time. He gave a paper at the TA Museum of Art. He said, à propos of nothing, "I met Honigman." I said, "So did I." He said, "She has such a wonderful face." I agreed. I don't know if you remember meeting him. He's a very gentle, lovely person. We talked about his obsession with mathematical theory. He's very good at math.

We later went to see an exhibit at the Japan Society by Hiro-shi Sugimoto, a photographer and collector of old things. It was called "History of History." My favorite part was a room of fossils. Sugimoto thinks fossils are like photographs.

Are you happy? Are you still in London? How are your kids? Sandro's in love with a girl named India.

I send you a kiss.

I've told almost no one about my relationship with the par-amour. In fact, the only two people who really know what's passed between us are my lover and myself. Of course, I guess you could say that about any pair of lovers. Sandro and Florence know a fair amount, and I've said enough to Walter that he's probably figured it out, or thinks he has. You know, he met her briefly at that PEN reading at Cooper Union. Every once in a while I'll find myself in an abstract conversation with someone about love, and I'll make oblique reference to "the paramour." But I never say who it is. I don't do this to create an air of mystery around myself. Of course, I do have a sense of humor about the ridiculousness of this code name.

I used to think that *paramour* must mean something approxi-mating, and yet distinct from, love. I figured the etymology was probably *para* (next to, or beyond, as in *paraphrase*, or *paramilitary*) and *amor*. But it turns out it's from the French *par* (by) *amour*. It goes straight through the heart of love. Oh well.

Anyway, as I was saying, when I make reference to "the par-amour," I'm kind of making fun of myself. It makes it sound like I have a secret and exciting love life. I guess I do, from a certain perspective, but as you can see, in most respects it's as stupid, awkward, and frustrating as anyone else's. I never use any terminology that would appear to ascribe specific terms to our relationship.

Tzipi, on the other hand, has sporadically used this kind of language in reference to me. It kind of irks me, because she never asked me if this was all right. As I told you, even when she was with Hannah she tended to be discreet about her private life. But periodically, she'll haul off and blab to somebody about me. I didn't worry when she told me she'd talked to Asher. He, like Sandro, has excellent judgment – much better, in fact than Tzipi. But one day she told me that Hannah had been hectoring her about me, and that she had asked Tzipi outright if I were her new "official girlfriend," and Tzipi, in an attempt to show defiance, had responded, "Yes, if you want to put it that way, she is."

When I heard about this exchange, I had profoundly mixed feelings. Obviously, I was flattered that Tzipi would even momentarily promote me to this lofty status. On the other hand, I saw four potential problems: 1. the designation was Hannah's, and Tzipi appeared to be embracing it mostly just to undermine Hannah's control; 2. given Tzipi's unpredictable and famously circuitous logic, this configuration could flip over at any given moment; 3. I worried, not unreasonably I think, that Hannah might come after me with a lethal weapon; and 4. I wasn't sure I *wanted* to be Tzipi Honigman's official girlfriend.

Once she'd said it to Hannah, however, she seemed to be on a roll. Even though I protested against the "girlfriend" line in an affectionately slighting e-mail (I said I'd prefer to be called her "concubine"), she almost immediately reported that she'd referred to me by name, in a conversation with another journalist she knew only vaguely, as her "lover." I didn't want her to think I was resisting being outed as her sexual partner for politically objectionable reasons, but given certain aspects of our relationship, I also thought she was overstepping a bit her rights of indiscretion.

Still, I confess, it gave me some small pleasure, for the moment, to feel loved. Of course, this little period of *da!* was quickly followed by yet another dose of *fort!*

I finished *The Mandarins*. Although Simone dedicated it to Algren, his character, "Lewis Brogan," occupies a surprisingly small number of pages in the book. He doesn't even appear until page 324. The sixth chapter is narrated in the first person by "Anne," the middle-aged French psychologist who falls for him when she goes on a trip to Chicago. At first, she seems a little calculating.

A couple of chapters later she reunites with her lover and they go on a trip to Mexico. He seems to resent the fact that she won't give up definitively her life in Paris with her left-wing intellectual husband. Still, there's a lot of chemistry between them. They keep breathlessly saying things like, "I'll love you till the day I die." At one point he says he's trying not to love her so much and she tells him to stop trying. It's melodramatic, and a little embarrassing.

Then in Chapter 10, she goes back to visit him again and he's chilly and distant. She's supposed to spend the whole summer with him, but he immediately announces something along the lines of, "I love you but I'm not in love with you." Interestingly, it's right around here that she says she's reading *The New Yorker* and suddenly thinks, "I don't give a damn about Faulkner – the real tragedy is that Lewis and I should be fucking and we're not." I paraphrase, but the business about Faulkner is really there.

Despite his new chilliness, "Lewis" thinks they should just go ahead and make the best of a bad situation, but "Anne" seems to flail between utter calm ("'Well, that's it,' I thought coldly.") and frightening despair ("I wanted to howl until I died.") When they part, they both seem to know it's over, but they agree that each will always have a place in the other's heart.

As you can imagine, the passionate parts feel badly overwritten. The interesting moments are the ones where both of them are being so chilly. The book ends with "Anne" contemplating suicide, but not because of losing "Lewis," and it isn't even because of war and the bleak fact that everybody dies anyway. It's because those things don't particularly move her anymore. But she doesn't kill herself. She thinks there's some vague possibility she'll be happy again some day. Very existentialist.

Here's a bit of a message from very early in our correspondence:

Tuesday, January 25, 2005, 8:16 p.m.
Subject: Mrs. S

You mention Simone de Beauvoir in your third book, but I'd already made the stylistic connection from the first one I read. I also discovered her when I was 17. (I read Une mort très douce on a trip to Paris with my mother. We thought at the time that she was dying, but she got better.)

Do you remember that Monty Python episode in which Mrs. Premise and Mrs. Conclusion go to visit Jean-Paul Sartre in Paris? "Mrs. S." says, "He's in one of his bleeding moods: 'the bourgeoisie this is the bourgeoisie that...'"

She did remember.

Once the paramour wrote me an e-mail that ended very affectionately, saying that it seemed I would be my lover's "friend forever or something like that." I answered, "Of course I am your friend forever." I hope I will be. Naturally, I am starting to wonder about the possible repercussions of writing this manuscript. I haven't received any word in over a week. The last message I sent was friendly, but I did mention something about Simone de Beauvoir's letters being "silly and brilliant and girlish and superior and pathetic and sadistic and loving and cold." This may have come across as somewhat accusatory. I think at this point it's hardly necessary to point out that I was also talking about myself.

Tzipi has the admirable habit of maintaining friendly relations with many of her former lovers. I've also tended to do this throughout my life. In fact, just this week I received an e-mail from someone I saw in my twenties. Ten years later, after Carlo and I split up, I called this person, and we had a brief and torrid repeat encounter. It was very helpful. It got me over the hump. Now, after another ten years, he was just checking in. It wasn't clear whether he would be interested in going to bed again. I do this kind of thing sometimes with my exes.

The other day I was flipping through the new *New Yorker* and I saw a picture of Mikhail Baryshnikov in an advertisement for a Movado watch. I looked at his face and thought, "He also breathed hotly and hungrily into Tzipi's mouth." They had a well-known and long-running, sporadic love affair years ago. In fact, there's a character very clearly based on him in her fourth novel, *With Conviction and with a Rigorous Sadness*. Now they're just friends. They kiss on the lips when they see each other, but in that friendly way you can do with someone after so many years.

Once I wrote Tzipi about a comment that a friend had made at a dinner party at my house. Sandro had entertained the guests by playing piano and making some uncanny jokes, and then he had passed out on the couch. My friend looked at me with his eyebrows raised and asked, "How did you create this miraculous person?" I said, "Well, I had an egg and I got some sperm." I was very proud, of course. I told you, Tzipi is also very close to her older son, Asher. She had told me that when she was trying to get pregnant with her ex-husband, they'd been living right near the beach and she had this sense that the pounding of the waves was part of the whole amniotic process of Asher's conception. After I wrote her about my friend Leonard's comment about Sandro, I mentioned one other lovely thing that Sandro had done, which particularly charmed Tzipi. She sent a quick message reiterating my friend's praise, and I responded:

Saturday, October 27, 2007, 10:16 p.m.
Subject: conception

> How did you conceive this miraculous person?

Right?

But it's very interesting that you changed the question a little bit. Leonard said, "How did you create this miraculous person?" "To create" is different from "to conceive," which would seem to imply that it's all about DNA, except "conception" also brings us back to Asher who was conceived in an atmosphere of sea-sex, which takes you far from both the behaviorist and the biological models.

But conception is a great word because it makes a child seem like a parent's IDEA, and that makes me think of the birth of Athena, who just popped out of Zeus's head.

I believe a little bit in biology and a little bit in behaviorism and I also believe I imagined Sandro and he popped out of my head fully formed, but I believe just as much in other highly unlikely explanations like reincarnation, or better yet, the aboriginal belief in child spirits and the woman's capacity to conceive alone depending on the strength of her orgasm and vaginal fluids.

I read about some people somewhere, I don't remember where, who thought that semen could last many years in a woman's body, so paternity could be attributed to a lover from her distant past. I find this interesting because sometimes I see in Sandro qualities of different people from my past, and it seems almost like all that semen mixed together. I like this idea.

But Sandro's theory is that he was very lucky to be "fathered" by my "lesbian friends" and by a "crazy Mexican" (Raul).

Are you still in Greece? I wanted to get back to Freud and "A Child is Being Beaten" and the masturbation of little girls.

We went to the Metropolitan Opera last night to see Verdi's Macbeth! Very bloody!

As you can see, things Greek have occupied a considerable amount of space in my correspondence with Tzipi. Which was part of why it was so important to me that we were going to be spending time together on Mykonos. In fact, the visit itself seemed to me so symbolic, even the most banal practical details – my connecting flight on Olympic Airlines, paying my cab fare to the driver, Epifanio – seemed to take on mythic significance. This was also attached to the fact that so many of the cultural references we had were fundamentally about sex and sexuality: Sappho, of course, and *Dionysus in '69*. We'd essentially been living in the mythic realm, or working our way toward it, and this is why, on that balmy night on Mykonos, it seemed oddly right that when I opened my eyes on Tzipi's guest bed to see who was entering the patio door, I saw Medusa.

She was carrying a boom box. Between this and the wriggling snakes all over her head, she was having a somewhat difficult time getting through the door. She banged the doorframe with her sound system, which was what really got my attention, but somehow she managed to get in, set up her equipment on the floor, and hit play. It was Fani Drakopoulou singing "Thelo na ta pio." Melina's snakes were dripping all over her forehead as she shimmied and swiveled to the music. Snakes in her eyes and the dim lighting may have contributed to her inability to discern that she was dancing for her arch nemesis, me, and not the impossibly desirable Tzipi. Her eyes were shut, in fact, and yet from her grimacing mouth and tremulous dance performance, it was clear that she was crying, and had been for some time. Aside from the snakes, Melina was wearing a flesh-tone Lycra unitard. Her large, firm breasts pushed up against it, struggling to escape. She had no panties on and her pubic hair was entirely visible. She swiveled her hips and turned in a circle, one snake slipping off her shoulder and dropping to the floor. Tzipi was right about her ass.

As you can imagine, things started to go haywire pretty quickly. The snakes weren't cooperating, and the CD started to skip. Melina, who was really in no condition to deal with these frustrations, ended up dropping to the floor herself and kicking the boom box with her left foot. Then she began sobbing and kicking away her snakes.

That's when her dad came thumping in, screaming in Greek. I couldn't tell if he was angrier with Melina or with me, and I didn't understand a word he said. All I know is, when Melina figured out I wasn't Tzipi, she started in on me too, and then she and her father started hitting each other, and the only thing she could yell at me in English was, "Bitch! Go back to America!" And finally her dad dragged her out and she carried the boom box and he managed to round up the snakes (in point of fact there were only five although their initial effect gave the impression of there being many more) and they were out of there. Fortunately I'd kept Epifanio's card and I called him and got him to take me back to the airport and after a hellish wait at the Olympic Airlines counter I managed to change my tickets and get the hell out of Mykonos. I had a splitting headache.

Don't look at me if this story seems overdetermined. Everything about my affair with Tzipi has been overdetermined. But in the aftermath, we did have an interesting exchange about Freud's essay, "Das Medusenhaupt," and Hélène Cixous's "Le Rire de la Méduse." Tzipi was interested in the figure of castration, and the thesis of the proliferating phalluses, of course, but she really has no patience with the notion of *"écriture féminine."* She had also forgotten that Freud suggests that petrifaction symbolizes "the comforting erection."

When I testily mentioned having had to pay a surcharge on my ticket to come back early, Tzipi did offer to reimburse me for the whole failed trip. I should also mention that Djeli ended up paying my Bamako hospital bill.

I realize that I will appear at least as hard-hearted as Tzipi for submitting Melina's anguish to this treatment – first a distanced irony, and then a clinical, psychoanalytic diagnosis highjacked for French feminist theoretical ends. The truth is that when I saw her slumped over on the floor in that ridiculous get-up come undone, the shadow of her hungry pubic hair and her mashed nipples urgently forcing their reality through her unitard, when I heard her moan and uselessly thud her foot at her uncaring snakes, when I watched her wipe the snot from her nose and grimace in all her exquisite pain, I felt for her, just as I felt for Hannah there on that sidewalk in Tel Aviv, as she clawed at her own arms and howled in agony. I may be a little more understated, but what is this but my own grim display of the intolerable ache of losing Tzipi Honigman? What are these little glimpses of our story together but "luminous spots to cure eyes damaged by gruesome night"?

Fortunately, I never lost it like this with the paramour. I told you, Tzipi was the one I fell in love with. She's the one I thrashed over, sobbed at, howled for, in my own quiet way.

I'm not in love with my lover. My ex-lover. I'm not sure what term to use. The paramour is my friend forever or something like that.

* * *

The following was actually the complete e-mail I sent Santutxo about Darwin. As I read it over, I see why I abbreviated it before. You may find some of it objectionable, on the grounds of certain sweeping generalizations about gender and writing. It's also pretty unbearably politically lofty. How embarrassing. I was responding to one of Santutxo's more excessive tirades, in which he'd careened from extremes of feminist speechifying to sexist hissy-fit, the apotheosis of which was a very tasteless joke about the female anatomy. He was irked by the fact that I'd attributed one of his more idiotic comments (about the French elections) to his own gender.

Saturday, June 9, 2007, 4:08 p.m.
Subject: Darwin

Fine, your idiocy is yours and yours alone, it's not because you're a man. But then I want you to admit that my aburrimiento and my meretricio are also mine alone and not because I'm a woman.

You think you're different (Swedish Basque, homo/heterosexual, right wing leftist, Darwinist feminist...). I also think I'm pretty unusual. Maybe it's a lot of egotism on both our parts. But of course I agree that we are (we should all be) experimental.

I understood when you said that your political posture vis-à-vis sex seemed arbitrary, the team you were rooting for. But I still think, even if we know we might be mistaken, we should always be looking for a more humane way of living (sorry, I know, this sounds like something Ségolène would say). But I'm serious. Maybe there is no perfect political system, and no perfect relationship between a man and a woman, but it doesn't have to be that horrid scenario in your lame joke.

They also say that adolescents are necessarily a pain in the ass, that they have to fight with their parents. Sometimes Sandro asks me, "Do you think I should stop calling you mom and just tell people you're my friend?" And I ask him why I can't be his mother and his friend. He agrees but he says that people assume that mothers and sons drive each other crazy.

I am and I want to remain your friend.

I loved the story of your neighbor the "old maid," and your identification with her, and the birth of your feminism. When I say you're Ultra-Sensitive, that's what I mean. It's your empathy. And that's why I'll always identify with the left: it's a politics of empathy. Maybe sometimes it's off track in the grand scheme of things, but it's based on this, the possibility of identifying with the other, and especially the more vulnerable.

There is no happy nation, but I believe that unjust societies are sadder. It's pure Hegel – the master is as enslaved by slavery as the slave. It's the same thing between men and women.

You told me more than once about that thing your Italian woman friend said, that we all want sexual liberty but the tendency is to want to deny liberty to the other. I don't agree.

You propose another formula, which I also find suspect (Freudian or not) – that all men want to love and all women want to be loved. I find it difficult to believe that anybody doesn't want to be loved.

That's why we create (compose, write, paint...). My artist friend Raul says, "It's all about the pussy." It's a joke, but it's true that it's at least partly about a desire to be loved. I agree with you that Che wanted to construct something much more important than happiness, and I agree that men have a tendency to think this way, beyond the present, way beyond. Maybe there's also an "all about the pussy" aspect, in the vulgar sense, and in the psychoanalytic sense of a desire to be loved by the mother. But that noble thing that goes WAY beyond the present, that also exists.

I've been thinking a lot about Shakespeare, because of the book you gave me, and because we went to see Hamlet. Well, obviously, that went way beyond the pussy in any sense you might take it.

It's less typical to find a woman making art at this level of ambition. The creative act tends to be more personal. Which doesn't necessarily make it inferior, but the tendency is often more modest. I write as a woman. Happiness is a priority for me. I don't find that better or worse. I just think I'm lucky.

I'm worried about your insomnia. You wrote me at the hour when I was waking up, and I think you still hadn't gone to bed. Sleep! It's one of the secrets to happiness.

Didn't I tell you what Florence said about typographical errors? Typos are sexy!

Santutxo had said in his message that aside from his inability to sleep or to be happy, aside from the insufferable, bellyaching rhetoric of Ségolène, aside from my own half-baked socialist idealism, aside from the pervasive whininess and unnecessary drama of my sex, the worst thing was that he'd reread a recent message he'd sent me and realized that he'd made an egregious number of very stupid spelling errors.

I'm not the only one who struggles with the paramour's incongruous and often irreconcilable opinions. Can you understand that I find Santutxo's profound commitment to feminism and the anticolonial struggle even more moving because of his occasional expressions of oafish sexism and racial and cultural insensitivity? He really does possess an uncanny ability to identify with the Other, even if that means subverting the most fundamental aspects of his being.

You may just think I've been buffaloed, but without those long and tortuous arguments over coffee and cigarettes back at UNAM, surely his most dedicated student would never have been able to come up with this:

"Marcos is gay in San Francisco, a black in South Africa, Asian in Europe, a Chicano in San Isidro, an anarchist in Spain, a Palestinian in Israel, an indigenous person in the streets of San

Cristóbal, a gang member in Neza, a rocker on campus, a Jew in Germany, ombudsman in the sedana, feminist in political parties, Communist in the post-Cold War era, prisoner in Cinalapa, pacifist in Bosnia... Marcos is every underrated, oppressed, exploited minority that is resisting and saying 'Enough!'" – El Sup, "Shadows of Tender Fury," 1995.

Massimo De Angelis dubbed this Marcos's "subversive affinity," but it's pure Santutxo – excepting that Santutxo also has moments when he identifies with Nancy Reagan. Naturally, Marcos gets frustrated with his friend, and so does Garzón – but to know Santutxo is to love him. If you knew him like I know him, you'd see what I mean.

Of course not everybody feels this way. Certain members of the ETA-M, for example, think he's an ass. And that was the reason, as you will have surmised, that I found myself that night in the stranglehold of that scabrous bald guy with the pierced lip.

"So, Tubal, look at what we've got here," said his swaggering, mohawked comrade. "This is the Txotxolo's little *andragai*." She hocked up a wad and spat in the general direction of my feet. I stared at the impressive glob of slobber on the floor. "Well, little American piglet, let's see how much your traitor boyfriend really cares for your little American piglet ass!"

My captors dragged me, struggling, out the back door of the so-called "safe" house. Waiting out back were two more thugs – a short, stocky heavy-metal guy with a bandana tied around his forehead, and a tall, beautiful, young woman with a conspicuous burn scar that stretched from her left cheek down into the deep V of her black V-neck sweater. They wordlessly ground out their cigarettes under foot and joined us in our bungling, contentious march across a small field toward the barn. Since none of us spoke, the only sound was more of those little dried sticks crackling under their boots. I was really regretting having worn high heels, but how could I have known?

The moon was nearly full, and out there in the country the stars speckled the sky like the pock marks on Tubal's ugly mug. There was a smell of fresh air, manure, and distant smoke.

When we got into the barn, the mohawked ringleader told Tubal to take me up to the loft. She and the others would go back to the house to make a couple of phone calls. Tubal dragged me up some wooden steps toward an enclosed loft. I snagged my thigh-high stockings on the way up and gave a little yelp. That pissed him off. "*Cállate*, American bitch! Nobody'll hear you out here." We'd reached the loft. He shoved me into a broken, old arm chair and shut the door. I was trying to keep my cool. Tubal and I stared defiantly at one another. He grabbed a hunk of chorizo that was sitting on a plate on a small table. Tossing it into my lap, he snarled, "Nobody's going to hurt you – you'll be out of here in an hour if your old man comes through. Now make yourself at home – but shut up!"

I was gnawing on my hunk of chorizo when, a few minutes later, we heard a rustling noise below, out in front of the barn. Tubal opened the shuttered window of the loft and looked down. Apparently he saw two men poking around the entry to the barn. "Hey," Tubal shouted in irritation, "what're you doing here?" That wasn't a very bright question, but to tell the truth, Tubal didn't give you the impression of being the brightest bulb.

I was later to learn that the men rustling around in front of the barn were a couple of Garzón's hired henchmen. They weren't cops – Garzón clearly couldn't let it get out that he was protecting the Arrano Beltza's lover – and I have a feeling they were the kind of men who would have played on anybody's team for the right price. Still, I'm very glad they ended up on mine. "Hey!" Tubal shouted again.

He rigged the door to the loft shut with a length of rope and clattered down the stairs to confront the intruders. I struggled with the rope on the door and managed to pry it open a couple of inches so I could see what was happening below.

Tubal was lumbering toward the two men like a zombie. I screamed. Tubal looked over his shoulder irritatedly.

"She's up in the loft!" one of them said.

"No way you're getting up there!" Tubal shouted threateningly.

"Well," said the other guy, "it's better to have loft and lost than never to have loft at all."

That's when the free-for-all started. Tubal was chasing the guys around in circles. Hay was flying everywhere. The chickens started squawking. Two horses watched the action with expressions of boredom. A cow bellowed.

The first hired man took a dive into a haystack, and the second man and Tubal followed. All I could see were sprays of hay shooting up into the air. Suddenly, Garzón's third man came running into the barn with a pitchfork. He ran over to the *lucha libre* in the haystack and poked poor Tubal in the ass.

"*Mierda!*" he shouted, turning to encounter the new threat. He was busy fending off the pitchfork when, to my great relief, Santutxo came running in.

"I'm up here!" I shouted. Santutxo looked up at me with – I swear to you – pure compassion and affection in his eyes. He ran over to Tubal and socked him in the neck. Tubal fell down and Santutxo came running up to the loft.

He'd finished untying the rope from the door and we had a quick embrace when suddenly the other three ETA thugs came running into the barn. Now it was going to get really hot.

Santutxo yelled from the loft, and all eyes turned up to him. The mohawked ringleader had her hand on the pistol tucked into the waistband of her jeans. "Okay," she said threateningly, "which one of you is the 'Arrano Beltza?'" Her voice dripped with bitter irony as she pronounced Santutxo's once proud *nom de guerre*.

With the fire of righteousness burning in his eyes, chin thrust forward, Santutxo intoned, "I am the Arrano Beltza."

There was a pause.

And then Garzón's first hireling, a goofball with a grease-paint moustache, a swallow-tail coat, and a cigar, stepped forward, saying, "I am the Arrano Beltza." And then the kooky Italian with a pork-pie hat stepped forward, saying, "I am the Arrano Beltza." And then the guy with the pitchfork, an angelic blond lunatic, stepped forward and honked a bicycle horn. Because this wasn't really a remake of *Spartacus*. This was the last scene of *Monkey Business*.

When the shock had settled on us all, Santutxo took a head-long dive from the loft into the fray. He landed directly on top of the ringleader. Garzón's men joined in and once again the hay was flying. The beautiful woman with the burn scar rose up momentarily, and the loon with the horn bonked her over the head – out cold. The thug with the bandana revived, briefly, only to get bonked himself. Santutxo was having a genuine fisticuffs with Tubal, and the moustachioed mercenary started clanging on a cowbell as though this were a boxing match: "Now they're in the center of the ring, and the crowd ROARS!…" And a cow mooed.

That's when Garzón himself came charging in, and the story was over.

Friday, April 18, 2008, 2:01 p.m.
Subject: religion

Everybody thinks Obama looked weaker in the last debate, but it was also because Hillary came out swinging so he was in the defensive position the whole time, which is always the weaker position. Take a little piece out of that, put it on the Yahoo! home page and it looks even worse. But it's true, she looked better this time. This doesn't convince me that she's the better candidate, just that she really wants to win.

I know you're not exactly in the anti-religion line of Marx. You're getting close but you were always more complicated than this. Somewhere in between this, Dionysus, and your friend Cornel West. Me too. I've been interested for a long time in various religions because of the political, ethical and aesthetic possibilities they offer. Liberation theology, of course, the Black Church, even spiritism fascinates me. But I always feel better when I see in the people connected to these things a tiny hint of ironic distance, something that shows that even though they believe, they know it's a fiction.

It's like that fiction I told you about, the fiction of being in love. Maybe it's not a necessary fiction, but it can be pretty productive. Which is more or less your friend's argument.

But living in this political climate here, where everybody has to keep repeating he or she is a Christian the whole time, it makes you a little queasy over the topic.

When I said that the article about the girl in the Abu Ghraib photos was moving, I should have said it was disturbing. Deeply. It just shows you how dehumanizing war is.

She's a lesbian, everybody says she was extremely sweet, very innocent. She's also monstrous. She went over there, participated, wrote about it, wrote e-mails to her girlfriend saying first that it was funny, then it got worse, she got disgusted, she wrote saying that she couldn't take it any more, that it was a nightmare, she started documenting the nightmare, but always with that adorable smile as if it were a picnic in the park, that "thumbs up" – it shows you something about photography, something about war, maybe something about women as soldiers.

The most disconcerting thing is the photographs. She looks so adorable and sweet.

Those young anarchists you mentioned sound a lot like Sandro and his friends. Very free. Sandro also wants to have an adventure with that 58-year-old friend of mine, the beautiful one. If she wanted it he'd do it in a minute along with another friend of his, boy or girl. When you wrote saying that this was "very important," I didn't understand if it was because they represented a new political moment you see emerging, or if it was important as a liberatory experience in your erotic life. Maybe both. It's good to feel free.

I think I told you, Sandro's friends keep sort of jokingly inviting me to join their party. But that's a little too close to home. I am going dancing with them though. The iPod rave is tonight!

As you can see, this was a fairly recent exchange we had about Obama and Clinton. Santutxo was enthusiastic about Obama from the get-go, but, as is his wont, he's had a couple of unpredictable moments of jumping ship. For a minute there he got a McCain bee in his bonnet, but fortunately that was short-lived. Of course he'd love to see a woman president, and there are many things he likes about Hillary, but he's very bothered by the fact that she'd be coming in on the coattails of her husband. He hates the idea of a dynasty. Bush II has been more than enough.

He got caught up in the skirmish between Hillary and Obama on religion when it showed up on the Yahoo! homepage. I have to undo a lot of nonsense from Yahoo! I had said that I thought Obama had a hard time concealing his own intelligence, and he probably really did believe on some level that religion was the opiate of the people. And I said I also thought that was true and I knew Santutxo believed the same thing, or something approximating it. Santutxo grudgingly conceded that, indeed, he believed something like that, even though, at this point in his life, he's disinclined to align himself directly with a Marxist truism.

I did end up going to the iPod rave with Sandro and his friends. It was great. A thousand people turned out in Union Square, each one dancing to his or her own beat. And yet we were also kind of dancing together. I found it very beautiful. Every once in a while somebody would invite you to hear their music, or want to hear yours. I shared for a while with a Jamaican guy, and, briefly, a German techno tourist.

Antonin Artaud loved the Marx Brothers. He said that the moments of "boiling anarchy" in their films represent nothing less than the essential poetic disintegration of reality. When a lady topples over a sofa, or some goon whacks a musical rhythm on his dancing partner's behind, "these events comprise a kind of exercise of intellectual freedom in which the unconscious of each of the characters, repressed by conventions and habits, avenges itself and us at the same time."

I never found out what "very important" meant. Maybe it was enough that I said it was good to "feel free." Santutxo suffered a lot in captivity. He still has nightmares. I told you, he's very afraid of dying.

CHAPTER 4: ON THE MOON

Let us take stock of the situation.

Something did happen, of course, between me and the paramour, and it involved a purloined letter. But the various versions I've given you are all fictional – obviously. That pseudo-Faulknerian account of the hallucinatory fever in the Bamako clinic was particularly implausible. Dengue fever has an incubation period of four to seven days. It couldn't possibly have happened the way I wrote it. Binh never could have risen to the top of the art world heap on the basis of such juvenile work as the "Nocturnal Emissions" series. I'm sure I don't need to point out the excess of the scene with the snakes, or the one from the Marx Brothers. By the way, you earlier probably should have noted the unlikelihood of somebody like Santutxo being able to get a visa to come to New York to visit me and have dinner with Slavoj Žižek. I narrowly resisted using the other hilarious scene from *Monkey Business* to explain that one – the one in which each of the stow-away Marx Brothers attempts to pass himself off to immigration officials as Maurice Chevalier by singing that ridiculous song.

No, clearly, the catastrophic event precipitated by an undelivered message trapped in my spam filter wasn't an art scandal, or a tropical disease, or a run-in with a crazy stalker, or a terrorist kidnapping. But it was humiliating, scary, sad, and funny – and full of intrigue, in both the French and American senses of the term. I can't really tell you any more than that. And regarding the use of guidebooks for research: I suppose I should also apologize for that. It's probably pretty evident that this novel was constructed out of some fairly questionable knowledge gleaned from Google, a small, arbitrary stack of library books, a few Netflix DVDs, and my bin of sent e-mails. I'm clearly not an expert in Israeli political fiction, Basque separatism, experimental digital art, or Malian pop music. I now know a little about all these things, but not a lot.

When Simone de Beauvoir wrote *The Mandarins*, she really knew what she was talking about. Those were very thinly veiled portraits of herself, Sartre, Camus, Koestler, and their lovers and friends. And of Algren. The novel takes place almost entirely in the smoky Parisian cafés she used to hang out in, and a little in Algren's gritty Chicago digs which she also haunted. In a letter to Algren, Simone explained that the title referred to the traditional elite circle of Chinese intellectuals. She said that that was an allegory for her elite little circle of French intellectual friends. The novel didn't have anything to do with China.

Simone de Beauvoir did eventually travel through China, and she wrote a book about it, but she wrote Algren saying that that book "is not too good," and that she hadn't really put a lot into it.

She wrote that letter in January, 1957. By that time, her correspondence with Algren was very sporadic. In fact, this was the only letter she wrote him that year. The editor of the correspondence notes that he also only wrote once in 1957 – in December, "still despondent and nostalgic for the old Wabansia magic, for their life and travels together." Wabansia was the cruddy Chicago street he lived on when they were lovers. His building was eventually torn down.

Friday, October 21, 2005, 11:48 p.m.
Subject: moon

You had asked about the moon and I forgot to tell you. For a while it was spectacular, gawdy, and then for the last couple of days it disappeared below the horizon. Do you know why that happens? I was disappointed because I was waiting for it to come back full and naked and shocking the way it looked that night from your house. Like a white lady's belly.

The first time Djeli kissed me, it was on the terrace of his apartment in Montmartre. After that embarrassing incident with Mariam in Bamako, I went home, of course, and a few months later found myself with reason to be in Paris. He invited me to his house, and this time I had a feeling something like this might happen. I'd brought him a couple of things from New York – that inappropriate scarf I'd knit, the iPod holder, a book. He looked at the little collection of offerings on the coffee table and smiled at me. He didn't seem particularly put off by my disproportionate display of generosity. I think people give him gifts all the time. He said, "Let's go out on the terrace. I'll show you the view."

We stepped out there, and there it was. Not the view, which was indeed very beautiful, but sort of predictably so – a picture postcard version of "the city of lights." A little too clichéd to move you. The shocking, gorgeous, and obscene thing was the moon. It was full, white, enormous, and utterly exposed. We'd both seen it. We tried to make small talk but there was nothing to say. Djeli kissed my neck.

About ten minutes later we were fucking on his bed. I told him, "I was commenting to my friend Florence the other day that you were the most beautiful man in the world." Djeli smiled.

I've been feeling guilty about implying Nelson Algren was a second-rate novelist. Over the last couple of days, I finally read *The Man with the Golden Arm*. I'm somewhat ashamed to say that I considered watching the Otto Preminger film instead. It's the story of a junkie gambler who inhabits the "underbelly" of Chicago. The movie stars Frank Sinatra. The paramour's recollection of this film is primarily focused on Kim Novak's breasts. I've never seen it. Well, I didn't watch the film but I did read the novel, and I can't decide whether I think it's very good or not very good. It's both. It's hard-boiled and lyrical, naïve and incisive, hackneyed and utterly original. But it turns out it did win a prize: the National Book Award. People seem to forget this. In fact, it was the very first National Book Award. Algren also received some sort of medal from the American Academy and Institute. He apparently refused to go to the ceremony in New York at which he would be given the medal, saying, facetiously, that he had to attend a meeting of a Ladies' Garden Club back home in Chicago. He was famously pissed off about the Preminger film because he hardly made a dime off it. He was also, as I mentioned, famously pissed off at Simone de Beauvoir. He said to somebody, "She doesn't baby her privacy, does she?" People who look back at the train wreck of the end of his career seem to concur that a) Algren got a raw deal and b) he ended up in a ditch he'd dug for himself. This is pretty much the story of Frankie Majcinek, the hero of *The Man with the Golden Arm*.

Wednesday, July 27, 2005, 10:18 a.m.
Subject: cozy

So you were in London when the bombs exploded? And when they killed that Brazilian electrician? I hope your trip went all right, despite these things.

I was very happy to read that you're composing. I loved the idea of an album called "Peau." More electric guitar is good. I don't know a lot about it but I like that you're playing more. My son plays keyboards in a rock band at school. He's also a little out of it. The other kids in the band are all sons of aging rockers. I went with them to a Mötley Crüe concert. Can you imagine this? Me and two tattooed dads, bald with ponytails. And the boys in the band. It was really funny.

As I write, Sandro's playing Thelonious Monk. Beautiful.

I saw Bill T. Jones's dance company in Central Park the other day and now I can't think about anything else. I didn't love everything, but I found it very provocative. I think the big question he was asking was - what does it mean to dance solo, to dance a duet, or to dance in a corps de ballet in a time of an atrocious war?

The iPod cozy that looks like it's made of moss is for you.

I wrote this message, of course, between the Coca-Cola incident and the first trip involving sex. Djeli was just beginning to formulate the way he wanted *Peau* to sound. He was exploring more and more the distorted, painful, expressive capacities of the electric guitar – ironically, as his lyrics were becoming ever more sparely lyrical and delicate. As I've said, I hadn't really thought a lot about electric guitar, since that wasn't my musical formation.

That field trip to the Mötley Crüe concert was fairly hilarious. I don't know who felt more out of place – me, or Sandro. It was in Madison Square Garden. Somebody had snagged a skybox for our party. I tried to chitchat with the ponytailed dads. A guy brought in giant cups of soda for us, and potato chips, on the house. You know how rock concerts are. We were very far from the stage, but they have those huge video projections on the side. There were some women dancers with enormous, buoyant boobs making snarling faces at the audience. Tommy Lee rode onto the stage on a motorcycle and the crowd went wild. The biggest hit, which got the most enthusiastic reception, was their classic, "Girls, Girls, Girls."

Perhaps you know the lyrics to that one. They start out extolling the virtues of leggy, red-lipped beauties from the West Coast and the Northeast; then they reminisce tenderly about a certain sexual escapade in Paris, France. They manage to rhyme "*ménage à trois*" with "breaking those Frenchies' laws."

Their rendition of this little chestnut was accompanied by much snarling and gyration from the dancers. The dads drank their sodas and ate chips. So did the kids. So did I. I was wondering what we were doing there but thinking it was an educational experience for Sandro and me.

If you do any research on Nelson Algren, one of the first factoids that inevitably pops up is that Lou Reed was inspired to write "Walk on the Wild Side" after reading Nelson Algren's neglected novel of the same name. Mötley Crüe also recorded a song called "Wild Side," but it's unclear to me whether it was influenced by Algren, or even by Lou Reed. It does have one interesting line, though, which seems to have something to do with the art of correspondence: "Forward my mail to me in hell."

Anyway, as regards our own correspondence, you can see even in this early message that I was already feeling very lucky to be on the receiving end of Djeli's reflections on his creative process, and I wanted to share with him some of the thoughts I'd been having about life, art, and politics. I'm really not sure how much of an impression they made.

Of course, *Peau* has nothing to do with Mötley Crüe. It's an almost excruciatingly beautiful album. Djeli's voice is fragile, exquisite, Ultra-Sensitive, erotic. Djeli, if you're reading this, please don't be angry.

If the nightingales could sing like you, they'd sing much sweeter than they do.

In August of 1947, Simone de Beauvoir went on a trip through Scandinavia with Sartre. He was very popular in Denmark because of his philosophical debt to Kierkegaard, and the Dutch and the Swedes also seemed to have hard-ons for his grim, realistic view of things. Simone wrote Algren about this trip, and she affected a kind of bemusement about the way everyone was fawning over Sartre. Mostly, she described the terrain – particularly when they got to Sweden. She wrote, "My beloved Nelson, I write to you from your ancestral land." She described the grey sea, the rocky soil, and the uncanny, strange quality of the light. She said it looked like a lunar landscape.

She wrote Algren, "Would you like to be on the moon with me, darling, or would you be afraid?"

Algren took a while to write back. She complained, "I do not like not to have letters from you." She ended that one: "Feel how much I love you, please feel it just now, because just now I love you so much."

A little over a month ago, Djeli wrote me saying that he was writing a song with an explicit critique of the catastrophic US foreign policy of the last eight years, but that he didn't think it played into the facile anti-American rhetoric so prevalent in France. As you know, I'm more comfortable with that kind of rhetoric than Djeli is. Djeli said jokingly that even if I perceived this song as an attack on my nation, I could take it as sexually motivated, since I had on any number of occasions observed that he liked to launch into political tirades when he seemed to be sexually aroused. That was friendly of him. But the message wasn't one of those where he directly provoked me for my simple-headed political correctness. I agreed with everything he said. In his e-mail, Djeli made the astute observation that in point of fact, he wasn't anti-American: it was the Bush administration which was undermining the very American ideals that Djeli still found compelling. I wrote him:

Thursday, April 24, 2008, 5:43 p.m.
Subject: anti-american

You're right, Bush is very anti-American. Did you ever read Emerson? Do you like him? When I read him, I feel American. It makes me cry. Montaigne makes me delirious, I prefer him, but I recognize myself in Emerson. The Self-Made Man.

Anyway, this diatribe of yours wasn't one of those rants against me, or in friction with my politics. But that's okay, I'll give it a sexual value since you said I could. And being a Self-Made Man, I rub my American manhood up against yours, affectionately.

In the 50th Anniversary Critical Edition of *The Man with the Golden Arm*, the critic George Bluestone made this surprisingly sentimental assertion: "If, as Algren makes abundantly clear, morality is not to be found in the law, the church, in criminal ethics, in social struggle, in any normative standards for success, then where is the moral authority? Only in love."

* * *

I cried a little writing that last section. I wasn't crying about Djeli. Djeli moves me, of course – his heartbreaking falsetto, his warm, soft kiss under the naked moon, the way he sometimes tries to provoke me sexually through his political bombast – but all these things make me smile. They don't make me cry. The truth is, I was crying for Nelson Algren.

Thursday, January 17, 2008, 3:04 a.m.
Subject: - Gatwick Airport

I slept heavily, early, woke up early, walked on the beach. The sky was a little overcast. Packed in the afternoon. The flight to London was fine. But I have a huge layover now and that's why I'm here killing time by writing you a long message with insignificant details on my BlackBerry.

I thought you were more near than far this time. Sometimes very near, the way you noticed everything, like the way one of my eyes opens a little slower than the other. In those moments I felt very naked. But I liked it.

Uh oh. I just cried a little in Gatwick Airport. It's okay, as soon as I get home I'll see Sandro and he'll say something hilarious, and Florence will come over in the evening and convince me to drink a martini, and I'll feel happy. I have a piece to write. I have to read the new Roth.

I love our sex but sometimes I wonder if it's okay for you. Sometimes I get very focused on myself. I do this because I think that it gives you pleasure when I feel pleasure. But afterwards I wonder. It's very intense for me – that thing you do, when you're so attentive, that little pause you make, I imagine you're feeling what I'm feeling. It's different, something that's ours, I find it beautiful, but I don't know how it is for you. I get dizzy just thinking about it.

The strategic error was saying I cried a little in Gatwick Airport.

As I mentioned before, the paramour responded to this e-mail with a banal message about mosquitoes, and very shortly thereafter we were playing fort/da. I later learned that the phrase that triggered the cold spell was when I said I'd "cried a little." This made my lover feel boxed in. Actually, reading it over now, I can understand that.

But what I started out saying was this: I honestly don't feel like crying right now over the paramour. In fact, I'm feeling extremely placid about things. I told you, when I wake up, I just want to get back to thinking about Tzipi.

I've gotten attached in different ways to all of the characters in this novel. Everything Santutxo's been through fascinates me, of course, and he's the wackiest, politically. In spite of everything, I fundamentally believe in his integrity. Even when he behaves badly – maybe especially then – I still admire that. I have the most affection for him, I think. Djeli's so beautiful. How could you not be moved by the delicate sound of his kora, and by that voice? I realize I should be nervous about this, but I'm completely sexually fixated on Binh. Every time I start working on a section about him, I have to stop halfway through to masturbate on my bed. I touch myself imagining that .mov file of his exquisite hard-on coming to life. I imagine him imagining me touching myself. But Tzipi was the one I fell in love with. Right now, I can't really imagine a world in which she didn't exist. Of all of my lovers, she's the most beautiful, the most vulnerable, the most brilliant, the most pathetic, the most loving, the most sadistic – the one closest to and furthest from the paramour. The one closest to and furthest from me.

Yesterday I went back and listened to the original recording of "You Brought a New Kind of Love to Me" by Maurice Chevalier. It's very strange. Right in the middle he stops singing and goes into a kind of rap of the lyrics:

> If the nightingales could sing like you
> They'd sing much sweeter than they do
> Hmm... you brought a new kind of love to me.

> If the Sandman brought me dreams of you
> I'd want to sleep my whole life through
> (Heh heh) you brought a new kind of love to me.

> Oh, I know, I know that you're the queen, and I'm the slave
> And yet you will understand
> That underneath it all
> You're a maid, and I'm only... a man.

Even with his smarmy delivery, it's pretty stunning when he makes that little anti-slavery pitch.

Sometimes I write things and it's only after I sleep on them that I realize their obvious significance. This morning, for example, I woke up and saw the clear connection between the story of the beheading of Medusa, the fear of castration, and the decapitation of the dirty pictures that I send the paramour. Medusa is such a fantastic figure, because she represents both castration *and* a female abundant overcompensation for the absent phallus. I told you that even Tzipi was intrigued by Freud's assertion of Medusa's ability to turn men to stone as a sign of the "comforting erection." Some comfort.

Of course, I thought I was just cropping my head out of those dirty digital pictures in case my e-mails accidentally went astray. But the Medusa subplot suggests another possibility: that my missing head is not only super-phallic – it's also capable of producing the ultimate hard-on.

I know, I know, wishful thinking.

I just got an e-mail from the paramour. It was very warm. It even made reference to a particular breathtaking aspect of our sex. This made me feel both affectionate and a little guilty. Before getting this e-mail, I had planned to write: Well, it's been about ten days since I heard from the paramour and our love is looking to me like a dying houseplant. You know, the last message I'd gotten was just that short, disgruntled one about the shrink. But I wasn't feeling sad about the lack of contact. On the contrary, I was marveling at my own canny manner of handling this situation. I was really much more preoccupied with Tzipi. So the coincidental thing about this is the explanation for the silence. What prompted this e-mail was a brief message from me saying that a colleague had just written me something mentioning the paramour, not knowing, of course, that we were intimate. What my colleague said was very complimentary. I knew that this comment would be of interest, so I passed it on. Then I said, "I think you have slipped far away right now and maybe I'll just hear tiny things from you every once in a while but I want you to know I hope you are happy and when I think of you it's with great tenderness." I also said my writing was going very well. My lover responded humorously to the anecdote about my colleague, and wondered a little about what I'd said about distance, alleging not to feel overly far away, and explaining the gap in communication by saying, "I'm in love with my work right now." And then came that tender reminiscence, nonetheless, of our particular and lovely way of fucking.

You can see why this is a little ironic – because of course I'm also in love with my work right now, and more specifically, with Tzipi Honigman. I'm tempted to tell my lover, who claims, as you know, to enjoy hearing about these things. I'm still not sure I believe this entirely. I'd also mentioned in my message that ex-boyfriend who rematerialized after all these years. I don't know if I mentioned this to be cruel or to be kind. I think I meant to be kind. I really do think of the paramour with great tenderness.

In July of 1952, after things had already fallen apart, Simone de Beauvoir wrote to Algren: "It seems to me I put my love for you in a deep, deep freezer, and it will never get out of it, but never get rotten or dead, neither. And I'll live with this useless deep frozen love, which is no trouble at all anyhow."

Over the very last few warm days of autumn, 2005, Sandro and I went out to visit friends who had a beach house on the Jersey shore. We spent a couple of nights there and it was very beautiful. I wrote Tzipi from their house.

Friday, October 21, 2005, 11:48 p.m.
Subject: moon

You had asked about the moon and I forgot to tell you. For a while it was spectacular, gawdy, and then for the last couple of days it disappeared below the horizon. Do you know why that happens? I was disappointed because I was waiting for it to come back full and naked and shocking the way it looked that night from your house. Like a white lady's belly.

Sandro will be very impressed that you once met Jean Pierre
Léaud. Yesterday he came home with his pants soaking wet
and covered with sand because he'd decided to go to a de-
serted beach and reenact the last scene of les 400 coups
where Léaud runs into the ocean and gets his feet wet.

I send you a kiss.

Only Tzipi could possibly understand the way the moon
looked that night on her terrace in Neve Tzedek. We both saw
it. It was so embarrassing. She had smilingly fingered the useless scarf and iPod holder, glanced at the unnecessary book. She
took me out to show me the view. A breeze was blowing in off
of Banana Beach, and you could faintly hear the hippie drum-
mers banging on their congas in the sand. The wind was sweeping up Tzipi's gorgeous mane of hair, and she pulled it back and
twisted it into a knot. Then she stepped behind me, combed my
own long hair back with her fingertips, gently twisted it behind
the nape of my neck, and leaned in and kissed me warmly just
below my ear. She kept holding my hair up with her left hand,
and I felt her right wrap around my stomach. My sex was wet.
I thought I might faint. Ten minutes later I was breathing hotly
into her mouth on her bed.

Of course Tzipi knew Jean Pierre Léaud. They actually spent
about a week together on a friend's houseboat in the south of
France in the '70s. She said he was a little crazy, but funny. That
was when she still smoked.

I had an upsetting thought. I wondered if my corresponding figure in Simone de Beauvoir's life might not be Nelson Algren, but rather "the ugly woman," Violette LeDuc. It's astonishing how much Simone writes to Algren about this woman.

As I mentioned, they used to meet for lunch once a month. But Simone gives much more frequent updates about her activities, always describing how this woman weeps and trembles in her presence, can't bear to hear of her other love affairs, writes obsessively about her sexual fantasies of Simone in her diaries. Simone says of this writing in the diaries, "It is tremendously good." She says the ugly woman writes "a beautiful language," daring and frighteningly honest. As I also mentioned, Simone expresses disdain for most women writers, who are, she says, "a little too sweet and subtle." The ugly woman, she says, "writes like a man with a very feminine sensitiveness." Actually, that's a better description of the paramour than it is of me.

Thursday, December 27, 2007, 12:31 p.m.
Subject: girl talk

I'm worried about you. If you can, write me just to say you're getting better. Maybe you already left for Jerusalem to see your brother. Maybe you're all better, spending time with your family.

All good here. Yesterday was Oscar Peterson Appreciation Day around here, because he died Sunday night. I must have listened to "Girl Talk" twenty times.

Then in the evening Sandro and I turned out all the lights and put on The Clash and danced in the dark. That was fun.

We watched Spartacus here at home on the big screen. Fantastic. We went to see Persepolis in the movie theater. Is it playing there? You should take Pitzi.

Tell me if your fever's gone down.

Oh no. Someone just called to tell me about Benazir.

Last winter Tzipi got the flu and it turned into a nasty upper respiratory infection. It's difficult for me to imagine her sick, because she's so strong. She didn't write for over a week and I began to worry. Two days after I sent this message she wrote back weakly that she'd been "dead for the last several days." But the fever had broken.

The way she'd put it made me sad. And then I realized that my own message had been a little morbid, too. About Oscar Peterson having died, and then Benazir. Tzipi's strong as a horse but she is a hypochondriac. As you know, the paramour's afraid of dying. And in point of fact, at the age of 68, I guess it's realistic for Tzipi to be contemplating her own mortality. That night of our first intimacy, when she was fingering the scarf and the iPod cozy, I noticed that her hands were trembling a little. I wondered to myself if she was a little nervous, or just starting to get old.

Once, when she started going off about her discomfort at the thought of death, I told her that my prediction was that she would live to be one hundred and two. Longevity runs in her family. I told Tzipi that this was good, because that way, if we really did fall in love when I was sixty and she was eighty-three, we wouldn't be in a hurry. There would still be plenty of time.

* * *

In 1996, Subcomandante Insurgente Marcos issued a stirring communiqué which has since been widely quoted by his followers: "The face that hides itself to be seen. The name that hides itself to be named. Behind our unnamable name, behind us, whom you see, behind us, we are you. Behind, we are the same simple, ordinary men and women, we are repeated in all races, painted in all colors, speak in all languages, and live in all places... Behind us, you are us. Behind our mask is the face of all excluded women, of all the forgotten indigenous, of all the persecuted homosexuals, of all the despised youth, of all the immigrants, of all those imprisoned for their words and votes, of all the humiliated workers, of all those dead from neglect, of all the simple and ordinary men and women who don't count, who aren't seen. We who are nameless."

Perhaps you will chafe at the suggestion that the masking of my lover's identity has anything at all to do with politics. And you're right. In fact, the ugly truth is that it probably has more to do with celebrity. El Sup would be appalled. Sandro was just telling me that he was watching El Sup on YouTube, and that he said something brilliant about how in the capitalist West we all care more about movie stars and whom they've been fucking and what they've been eating than we care about the struggles of the common man. Some starlet screwed her bodyguard and ate a cheeseburger last night: fascinating. El Sup said that the only time we speak of the suffering of the peasants, it's when there's some huge natural catastrophe. It's true, right after the enormous earthquake in China a couple of weeks ago people looked up and said, oh, wow, 40,000 people just died.

Take a look at the Yahoo! homepage.

I realize this is all very self-indulgent. But you know, even Simone de Beauvoir got tired sometimes of thinking about politics. Her correspondence with Algren is full of these kinds of admissions. She'll say, "I feel it is very silly to give so much importance to one's own feelings when the world is so big and so many things happen: cholera in Egypt, de Gaulle in France, to say nothing about USA." But she says what she really wants to be thinking about is lying down again with Algren: "When I'll shut my eyes, you'll come. Take me in your arms, give me your mouth..."

Tuesday, September 26, 2006, 4:15 p.m.
Subject: defense of the left

I think I understood what you said about what you meant about equivocation, although it's confusing, because it's for and against it at the same time (equivocal about equivocation). You can be very confusing, which is what I love about the way you think. You're right when you say that I shouldn't say that we'll always disagree about some things – in fact, you change my ideas all the time – about politics, about cinema... Sometimes then I change my mind back. Sometimes I don't. I only get a little exaggerated like that in my attitude of "political correctness" (I hate it when you use this term) because I find it irritating when you categorically register your disillusionment with the left. Because that's not exactly the way it is. It's true that it's a problem when one loses subtlety or perspective. Or a sense of humor. But the other day I was watching a documentary with Sandro about Howard Zinn (you must know who he is – a great leftist historian, an activist from my father's generation). And an old colleague of his, a woman, said with a big smile, "It gives you so much satisfaction, to live the life of an activist, it's so pleasurable..." It's not all the left that's lost its sense of irony, or humor, or pleasure, or subtlety, and it's not all holier-than-thou.

Hurry up and come to New York. You would love some of our funny, self-ironizing leftist friends. And I would love to lie down next to you on my soft white bed.

I'm sending you two pure flowers.

I attached a picture of a pink morning glory from my balcony, and another of my nipple.

A year before the famous communiqué of the "nameless," El Sup wrote another called "Death Has Paid a Visit." It begins comically, noting that little pieces of his body keep falling off (chip off his shoulder, piece of thigh – will his nose be next? At least then the ski mask would lay flat...). But following his best sense of "guerrilla anatomy," he's been sticking them back on. This is his way of saying that he senses his own mortality. After some more surreal, politically trenchant and hysterical poetry, he modestly suggests that the government withdraw its arrest order against him, because since it was issued, "the Sup has been insufferable. And I don't just refer to his obsession with death." He's constantly looking over his shoulder. He's also started spouting weird pseudo-religious prophecies to his comrades, and sharing his plans for degenerate sex acts when he next encounters "a certain Monica or such-and-such Aimée." Everybody would be better off, surely, if he could get the murderous government soldiers off his tail. He signs his message, "THE SUBDELINQUENT TRANSGRESSOR OF THE LAW, FLEEING THROUGH THE HILLS, SUB MARCOS."

Last fall Santutxo and I started debating intellectual property rights. Given his politics, you might think that he would be a big open source enthusiast. Or maybe you would think the opposite. Surprise: he argues both for and against the fierce protection of copyright. Although he expresses strong opinions, he feels a little under-informed on the topic, so I was trying to bring him up to speed. I ended up reflecting a little on the patterns of our political discussions:

Thursday, September 27, 2007, 2:10 p.m.
Subject: politics and eros

Anyway, what I find fascinating about you is that even though the arguments we have are usually about race politics or sexual politics (you are less adamant about intellectual property rights so maybe we will have a real disagreement about this later but not yet), your ideas about both these things are still very complicated and interesting to me, and interrelated precisely in the realm of eros.

This is why I said of the Communiqué on Mortality that when you are talking about sex you are talking about politics, and vice versa.

I've exchanged a couple of e-mails with my friend DJ Spooky about intellectual property rights. But nothing that I think would illuminate things for you. He just sent me a track from his new album, where he took some drum solos from Stewart Copeland, the drummer from The Police, and reproduced them by splicing together digital beats so they sound like the original but they're not samples. He included a photo of himself with Copeland, Copeland holding Spooky's book and smiling with his fist in the air. I guess he liked what Spooky did with his solos. You might be appalled or you might like it, I'm not sure.

Fingerless gloves are good in cool weather when you still need to be able to use your fingers (to play piano or guitar, to hold a pen or pencil, to use a key or pick up a coin, etc.). They keep the cold wind from going up the sleeve of your coat. They make you look like a character from a Dickens novel. They can be very stylish. I could send them to you through Pablo.

I am happy. Sandro is so beautiful these days. I worry because he's working so hard. They have him learning violin right now, probably changing to bass later. Math is very hard for him. The girls are all over him. There are six that take him out every day after school and buy him cakes and sweets. It's a good thing he's congenitally skinny, and it's also a good thing he's a lesbian like you or he would be getting unbearable.

The only questions I asked you in my last e-mail were: 1. Have you read David Graeber? 2. Can you tell me the alternative address where it's safe to send a package? I'm not asking again if you want fingerless gloves because I think you don't but I am hard-headed and may make them for you anyway.

XOXO

Although Sandro went through that period of hanging out with a whole gaggle of girls who wanted to feed him, he ended up getting a particular girlfriend whom everybody referred to as "Janis Joplin." They just broke up. She was a pretty tough customer. She was grumpy about several things, including Sandro's support of Obama. She prefers Hillary. She told Sandro she thought Hillary had a better position on gay marriage than Obama. Joplin, like Sandro, claims to be a lesbian at heart. But she had very little patience for his poses. She told Sandro, "You hide behind your Mayakovsky." By this, she apparently meant that he pretentiously trots out his list of avant-garde and left-wing enthusiasms, but fails to research the basic issues. Of course, she's right, but it's the kind of flaw a person could find either irritating or charming. Before they got in the fight, Sandro took this picture of himself kissing Joplin at National Pillow Fight Day in Union Square. I thought it was so beautiful, I sent it to Santutxo. I think he was also profoundly moved.

Sunday, March 23, 2008, 10:51 a.m.
Subject: Happy Easter

My trip went very smoothly. I slept six hours, then watched a bad movie (Nanny Diaries with Scarlett Johansson) and listened to Joan Armatrading on the iPod. When I got home, the apartment was a mess, covered with little feathers: yesterday was National Pillow Fight Day and there was a big party in Union Square. A thousand people hitting each other over the head with pillows. Sandro went with Janis Joplin. I attach a photo.

I love this picture, the two of them covered with feathers, and the cops behind them.

I vacuumed the whole house, started washing the dishes, and Sandro came in. Gorgeous. He'd grown (I swear). He was so affectionate and sweet with me. He went out to get Chinese food and we ate it watching the Marx Brothers (Monkey Business). My brother came by around 10. He was arriving from the set of a gay porn film for which he'd been contracted to write the script. It sounded funny.

We went out on the terrace so he could have a smoke. The moon was out, but it was obscured by some clouds that looked like the scales of fish.

Sandro's playing piano as I write, improvising. Last night I went to bed at midnight, to the sound of him playing. I fell asleep smiling. I woke up this morning with a hard-on, thinking of you. It was that normal morning kind of hard-on. In men we call this "morning wood." Anyway, I missed our fucking, but then Sandro called me in for a little cuddle in his bed and I felt very happy. It's sunny in New York. I think today I'm going to buy some seeds to plant on the terrace.

Tomorrow we're going to the Bowery Poetry Club to see Clement read from Mayakovsky's poetry (there's a new book out about him). Clement sent me a hilarious e-mail in response to the invitation to Sandro's birthday:

>Right now the Nigerian mosque on Myrtle Avenue is ululating in honour of the

>Prophet's (upon him be peace) birthday, and it has caused the normally restive folk

>in these parts to become silent and meditative. I assume Sandro's mustering will

>have a totally dissimilar character.

>Only those proverbially riotous equines could keep me from such an assembly. I

>have only to find a monstrous and unacceptable gift.

>Petrified,

>CVJ

>p.s. "Janis Joplin"?

I wrote this message shortly after the last time we saw each other. And four days later, I wrote this one:

Thursday, March 27, 2008, 8:31 a.m.
Subject: Mayakovsky

Monday night we went to that reading of poems by Mayakovsky. Clement read in Russian and English. He was dressed like a fop, completely charming. There were several other readers - some actors, and some academics. It was in a poetry bar on the Bowery, and they projected beautiful photographs of Mayakovsky on the wall the whole time. Sandro was captivated, of course, and asked for a book of Mayakovsky's poems for his birthday.

When they recited that line from "A Cloud in Trousers" – "Mama, tell my sisters, Ljuda and Olja...," I remembered a poem I'd written when I was 21 in which I stole this line. I just found it. Will attach.

Sandro's playing piano so well it's frightening. Today's his birthday. 15, going on 70. I can't explain it.

Florence is great, back in town. We're hanging out this afternoon.

I need to start a new writing project I think, and maybe find a new lover. I'll see my ex next week probably but that's a little complicated.

And you, little frog, are you feeling less tired? Did you call the yoga instructor?

I did attach the poem. Here it is:

But We Were Led to Believe that We Were Going Somewhere

Yesterday we left for good. We climbed
Into a great fish, and took our seats behind
Its fat, red heart. Through the fish's skin the sea

Looked green. We watched the telephone poles skip by,
And the wires stretch out like muscles along the air.
We are trying to derive our emotions now from bare

Cold places. I believe that you were right
About our lot. We will always be too late
For something – fumbling for our tickets, sick

At heart, and getting stranded on some dock.
Looking at each other. Feeling lost,
And calling home. "Mama. Tell my sisters,

Ljuda and Olja, that there's no way out."
There's no way out of here. You know that, don't
You? Damn it! We wanted so badly to arrive

In time. Now look at us: caught in this grave
And hostile, slanted light. "As for the future,
It doesn't belong to us either. I am sure

That in a few decades we shall be cruelly labeled
As products of the past millennium." They told
Us so. Oh, we really thought we were "someone."

We spent the whole night talking of things to come.

I cried a little during the writing of this section, but I was crying for Marcos, because he was afraid of dying, and also because Sandro broke up with Joplin.

* * *

It's coming to the end and so I allowed myself a chronological glitch. Sometimes when I knit things, I like to leave in a mistake or two, because it seems to make the project more personal. In case you didn't notice: I only taught the paramour the expression "morning wood" last March, which was after the purloined e-mail and the catastrophe, whichever version you choose.

For the most part, I've stuck with the actual chronology. I suspended a little the timing of the climax to allow for maximum flexibility, but naturally I've changed and added all kinds of details. This is a work of fiction. That was the point.

I've been composing in my head the cover letter I'll send with this manuscript when I mail it to the paramour. I want to make it as tender as possible. I realize I'm probably driving a nail into the coffin of our love affair. Still, I would like to be my lover's friend forever or something like that. I think that's really the most optimistic version of the 60-83 scenario.

Sunday, October 30, 2005, 11:17 p.m.
Subject: bruised

You said that your memory of the film was bruised, like a fragile membrane. Mine too. I think that's the quality that moved me. It has everything to do with the tango. A kind of hyper-sensitivity that's sexual and irritating at the same time. Frictive.

He made Happy Together in 1997, just before the government changed in Hong Kong, and some people at the time said that it was an allegory of the postcolonial state. A sick and exhausted love that expresses itself sometimes through violence. And neither side wants to give it up. Which also has to do with tango. And Argentina. Tango also has a complicated history of men dancing together. I found all of this interesting – principally because there are a lot of films about tango but for me none of them explores the implications (political, sexual, aesthetic) of the dance with as much subtlety as this film about two Chinese men in Buenos Aires. But the thing that stayed with me, to tell the truth, was that sensation of a contusion that you talked about.

I didn't see In the Mood for Love, which everybody says is so interesting. I liked 2046 which came out this year. Chungking Express and the other one whose name I forgot are very sexy and rapturous but a little bit MTV, which I think might bother you. 2046 is also very stylized in the way it's shot but there's enough that's complicated about the way he thinks about narrative time and obsessive love that it seems to merit all that excessive beauty. Also the beauty of the women. And Tony Leung, who is such a great movie star.

Of course it's hard for me to read this e-mail now and not reflect on my relationship with Binh. It would be dramatic and excessive to call this a "sick and exhausted love that expresses itself sometimes through violence." Even though everything began with that scene of Coca-Cola and tumult, the truth is that Binh and I are both very gentle people. You may remember that I told Tzipi that my aggression was generally of the passive variety. I think you could say the same of Binh.

But of course I also think about that postcolonial allegory. It's not uncomplicated that I'm American and he's Vietnamese.

I thought about visiting him in Hanoi. I think I mentioned, I was reading some guidebooks as research. But I ended up feeling that trip would just be too hard for me. It's that white liberal guilt.

Once I told Binh that I thought maybe it was good that in certain respects – like gender – he held the privileged position, while in others – like nation – I did. I'm not sure who held the privilege in age.

Last summer Binh flew down to Antarctica. Because there was no wireless or BlackBerry reception, we were out of contact for several days. He'd gone down there to collaborate with his friend DJ Spooky. Spooky was sampling the sound of the icebergs melting. Binh was going to help him shoot the digital images. Obviously, Spooky wanted to make a statement about global warming. In the YouTube teaser he made for this project before going down there, Spooky mentions that the Greeks made up the idea of Antarctica. They had formulated the idea of the Arctic from the constellation of Arktos (the bear), and figured there must be a corresponding ant-Arktos on the other end of the world. Spooky says, "They never actually went there, it was just a guess."

This is interesting because Simone wrote Algren that "on the moon" letter from the Arctic Circle, when she traveled to the north of Sweden with Jean Paul Sartre.

Tuesday, August 2, 2005, 10:28 p.m.
Subject: conceptual art

Yesterday morning a guy stopped me on the street. He was young and handsome, with an afro. He said his name was

Ben. He said that I was beautiful and he asked to take a picture with me. He gave his camera to a woman and asked her to take our picture. He embraced me as though I were his very close friend. He asked her to take another picture. He kissed me on the cheek with so much tenderness. In the picture, it's going to look as though I were the great love of his life. He thanked me. I don't know if he was crazy or if he was a conceptual artist. I liked it.

You said you hate cell phones. Me too. I only use mine to communicate with Sandro, because he goes out a lot on his own. My mother gets furious with people who speak loudly on cell phones on the street. When she came to visit us, she would pass these people and say, not very discreetly, "Shut up." I also don't know if my mother is a little crazy or a conceptual artist.

It's hot here. Sandro and I are starting to count the days until we go to Paris.

Look, this message was from very early in the correspondence. I picked it out because it says something about conceptual art. Although Binh is a conceptual artist, of course, the paramour is not somebody you would refer to in these terms. After I sent this e-mail, I was speaking to my friend Raul, who in fact *is* a conceptual artist, and I told him this same story of the guy with the camera on the street. I had found this a very touching encounter. But Raul informed me that this is the oldest trick in the book. Guys who do this, he explained, are generally pickpockets. They get you all close like this, and you're busy smiling for the camera, and they reach into your bag and take your wallet. That was disappointing. The good news is, the guy didn't actually get anything. None of my cash or cards was missing. I came out of the encounter entirely unscathed. And if Raul hadn't told me I'd been had, I would have gone on thinking that that guy might have treasured that photograph of us together for years, and it would have looked like I was the love of his life.

I wish he hadn't told me.

Speaking of the deceptive use of photography, this is the actual, uncropped photo from my early correspondence with Binh:

That's my hand, of course. I already told you that I'm the one who's been sending digital images as attachments all this time. So it should really come as no surprise that I, not Binh, was the one to proffer my heart on a plate. Interpret that as you will – but it's evident that there was again a bit of wishful thinking in attributing the gesture to my lover. Fiction affords the convenient possibility of switching things around. You could also ask yourself what it means that I insisted that Binh was an artist of genius, considering that I actually shot that uncanny still of my lazy eye with the antiquated little webcam. And I didn't even show you the one I took of my vulva. It's very poetic.

The titles of Tzipi's novels were also culled from my own unpublished manuscripts.

Nelson Algren similarly careened between self-effacement and self-aggrandizement. Sometimes it's hard to say whether it's one thing he's doing or the other. You could argue that he was the one who brought on his own obscurity at the end of his life. He certainly predicted it. They misspelled his name on his tombstone. But a few years before, he'd written that it didn't really matter having your name attached to anything, as long as it was inscribed "on some cornerstone of a human heart." He said, "On the heart it don't matter how you spell it."

The picture of my heart on a plate may have been misleading, but it doesn't really correspond to the photo with the con artist. The con artist doesn't correspond to me, or Binh, and in many ways Binh doesn't correspond to the paramour. Neither does Tzipi, or Santutxo, or Djeli. Simone de Beauvoir doesn't correspond to my lover, and I don't correspond to Simone, or Nelson Algren, or "the ugly woman." The paramour doesn't correspond to Zeppo Marx in *Monkey Business*, and I don't correspond to Tony Curtis as the "body slave." In fact, I don't really correspond to this narrative voice. Or I do, but I don't. There were many of us, or maybe we were just two. We were hardly elite Chinese intellectuals, or French ones – we just wanted to feel like we were for a little while, and it was romantic and it was sexy and I know I'm going to miss it. I mean I'll miss the fiction, I'll miss Tzipi and her cruelty and her hair, I'll miss Binh's strange images and his beautiful cock, and Djeli's angelic voice, and Santutxo's hypochondria. I'll miss waking up every morning and running to the computer so I could be with them again. And I cried a little, again, writing the end.

But your friends can always see this fiction for what it is from the outside, and they know that you could be happy again if you wanted to. This is almost exactly the way *The Mandarins* ends, but a little more "American" and less existentialist.

ACKNOWLEDGEMENTS

Thanks to: S. Calle (inspiration), H. Mathews and M. Chaix
(glass of wine and a Cuban); D. Levine (title); J. Taylor (notes);
E. Obenauf and E. Obenauf (even more notes); A. Pellegrini,
C. Smith, C. Swartz, A. Schnore, J. Lewis, J. Vaccaro, R. Enriquez,
and V. DeConcini (encouragement); L. Oliveira (misgivings);
E. Cowhig (maternal grace). Tzipi, sorry.

Also published by **TWO DOLLAR RADIO**

THE ORANGE EATS CREEPS
A NOVEL BY GRACE KRILANOVICH
A Trade Paperback Original; 978-0-9820151-8-6; $16 US
  * National Book Foundation 2010 '5 Under 35' Selection.
  * NPR Best Books of 2010.
  * Amazon's Best Science Fiction/Fantasy Books of 2010.
"Beautiful and deranged." —*Bookforum*

SOME THINGS THAT MEANT THE WORLD TO ME
A NOVEL BY JOSHUA MOHR
A Trade Paperback Original; 978-0-9820151-1-7; $15.50 US
  * *Oprah Magazine* Top 10 Terrific Read of 2009.
  * *The Nervous Breakdown* Best Book of 2009.
  * *San Francisco Chronicle* Bestseller.
"Mohr's first novel is biting and heartbreaking... it's as touching as it is shocking." —*Publishers Weekly* (Starred)

THE DROP EDGE OF YONDER
A NOVEL BY RUDOLPH WURLITZER
A Trade Paperback Original; 978-0-9763895-5-2; $15.00 US
  * *Time Out New York*'s Best Book of 2008.
  * *ForeWord* Magazine 2008 Gold Medal in Literary Fiction.
"A picaresque American *Book of the Dead*... in the tradition of Thomas Pynchon, Joseph Heller, Kurt Vonnegut, and Terry Southern." —*Los Angeles Times*

EROTOMANIA: A ROMANCE
A NOVEL BY FRANCIS LEVY
A Trade Paperback Original; 978-0-9763895-7-6; $14.00 US
  * *Queerty* Top 10 Book of 2008.
  * *Inland Empire Weekly* Standout Book of 2008.
"Miller, Lawrence, and Genet stop by like proud ancestors."
—*Village Voice*

THE PEOPLE WHO WATCHED HER PASS BY
A NOVEL BY SCOTT BRADFIELD
A Trade Paperback Original; 978-0-9820151-5-5; $14.50 US
"Challenging [and] original... A billowy adventure of a book. In a book that supplies few answers, Bradfield's lavish eloquence is the presiding constant."
—*New York Times Book Review*